KILLER WEDDING

A CHRISTIE'S FLOWER SHOPPE MYSTERY

PJ PETERSON

FINNGIRL, LLC

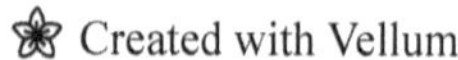 Created with Vellum

CHAPTER 1

"*S*tephanotis isn't exactly a tropical flower," Christie explained to Hailey, "but it is beautiful, and white and has been a popular choice to include in the bride's bouquet."

Hailey wrinkled her nose and tilted her head. "I was thinking something bigger and fancier than that little thing." She opened her wedding Pinterest page on her cell phone and pointed to a picture of a white lily. "Would something like this work?"

Christie resisted the temptation to immediately eliminate the strong-smelling bloom from contention—she hated to have to clip out the multiple orange-filled anthers of each one— saying instead, "If I use a lot of those lilies together, the fragrance can be quite over-powering. There are many other flowers that will give you that tropical look. Or I can use artificial stems that look very real."

"Oh, dear, no," said Michelle Starr, Hailey's mother, with a sneer. "We can't have anything but real flowers. I'm afraid the groom's mother would notice and make a fuss. Only the best, you see, for her precious Ryan."

Hailey rolled her eyes at her mother's snide tone.

"I get it," said Christie. "Fortunately, there are lots of other possibilities." She thumbed through the wedding flower planning book on the desk to look for photos of other large blooms. "Here's a lovely white mophead hydrangea. It would be quite dramatic." Michelle tilted her head, considering the idea.

Christie was about to show her yet another flower combination when she had an inspiration. "I have a better idea. Take some time here and look through this file with your mother while I take care of some business. When you see something you like, put a post-it note on the page. That'll make it easier to see what your preferences are. Then we can narrow it down by availability and cost and create a design plan."

Michelle smiled and said to her daughter, "That's a good idea, Hailey. It will help Ms. O'Mara to know your tastes better." She glanced at her watch. "We have about an hour before we meet your father for lunch at the country club."

Hailey scowled and huffed but gave in to her mother's wishes. Whether her attitude stemmed from the mention of her tastes or about the lunch, Christie didn't know. But then again, Hailey was at the age that Christie often found to be contrary for little reason. The young woman started flipping pages. Christie managed a smile with a clenched jaw and scooted her chair away from the small table.

The door chimed as Christie walked to her work counter, where Aunt Doris had laid a list of the blooms she needed from the wholesalers for the week ahead. She looked up to see her friend Anita saunter in, a big grin on her face.

Christie walked up to meet her and gave her a hug. "What a surprise to see you in here today. I thought you were headed to the beach with your family."

"Well, that plan changed because my mom's sister came down from Tacoma unexpectedly, and I offered to let her take my place in the car for the beach. I told her I had papers to grade anyway so she wouldn't feel bad about the switch."

"I'm sorry you're missing a beach trip, but why are you grinning like the Cheshire Cat?"

"I have a date tonight." Anita giggled like a teenaged version of her thirty-three-year-old self. "Guess who!"

"I have no clue since you haven't mentioned anybody interesting lately. Who's the lucky guy?"

"Well, his name is Nathan Starr. He's about forty and recently divorced."

Christie's eyes widened at the last name. She put a finger to her lips and pointed to Hailey and Michelle. Before she could whisper anything to Anita, she heard chairs scrape the floor behind her. She turned to see daughter and mother walking toward them.

"Did you say Nathan Starr?" Michelle asked Anita, a quizzical look on her face.

"Yes," replied Anita. "Do you know him?"

"Nathan's my husband's nephew," she said icily.

Stormy chose that moment to hop down from her perch. She sat on the counter directly in front of Michelle, hissed, and flicked her tail back and forth. Christie had learned this sign: her cat was unhappy about something.

Michelle stepped back, startled.

"I'm so sorry," said Christie. "Stormy can be moody at times." Christie picked up the kitty and put her back on her favorite perch, kissing her on the nose in the process.

Michelle put the portfolios on the counter where Stormy had been sitting. "Hailey marked some flowers that I hope you'll be able to work into the decor. I'll check with you in a couple of days."

"Of course," said Christie. "I'll need to order all the flowers no later than next Monday. Thanks so much for coming in."

Christie and Anita waited in silence as the pair exited the shop.

"Who are they?" Anita asked. "The older woman doesn't seem to like her nephew much."

Christie took a big breath. "That's Hailey Starr and her mother, Michelle. Conan Starr, the dad, is the big boss at the nuclear plant across the river."

"Oh, that might explain her attitude about Nathan. He works for the Nuclear Regulatory Commission."

"Well, that might be the reason." Christie shrugged. "Or not. You never know with families." Anita nodded. "Anyway, they've asked me to do the flowers for Hailey's wedding next weekend."

"Next weekend? As in just over a week from now? Isn't that kinda short notice?"

"Exactly. They were originally planning to use a shop down the road, but the florist canceled out on them a couple of days ago. Mrs. Starr said they had major differences of opinion about the design."

"And you've agreed to do it, it appears."

"Maybe against my better judgment but, yes, this is a big deal for me." Christie's eyes sparkled. "I've dreamed of doing the flowers for a big wedding even back when I was working for Grandma Maude. Nowadays, young brides seem to head to the bigger florists down the highway."

"I'm not sure Stormy is as enthusiastic as you are about working with them."

"I was surprised that she voiced an opinion." Christie finger-waved at Stormy, who peered down from her observation station. "Anyway, it'll be my first big wedding in White Castle, maybe even the wedding of the year. They want me to decorate the church and the country club. And make the bride's bouquet and the bridesmaids' corsages and boutonnieres for all the men. And the mothers, too. Corsages for the women, I mean." Christie clapped her hands together and grinned. "And they're willing to pay top dollar. It could be really good for business."

When Christie opened her flower shop a short six months ago, an unfortunate event (Christie preferred to think of it that way rather than as a murder—even though it was) had put the new business on the line. While her efforts had eventually cleared her shop of any implied involvement and solved the crime, people still occasionally referred to Christie's Flower Shoppe as "the Killer Flower Shop," much to her chagrin. If she could pull off this big wedding, it would be a boon not just to her dwindling bank account but to her reputation as well.

"That mom, Mrs. Starr, strikes me as perhaps a little difficult to work with," said Anita.

"So I noticed, but I only have to work with her for a few days, and I can use the money." Christie squeezed Anita's hands. "You'll help me, won't you, with the design? They want me to create the appearance of a tropical wedding, of all things."

"Of course, I'll help. It'll distract me from the craziness going on in my classes while I imagine myself heading to a lovely island vacation without them."

"And maybe with Mrs. Starr's nephew?" Christie teased.

Anita blushed.

CHAPTER 2

"Tell me more about Nathan while I fill out this order for the wholesaler," said Christie.

"Remember when I went to the sale at the school garden back in March? I was poking around the table where there were small pots of all kinds of flowers and vegetables, looking for geraniums and fuchsias to put in big planters on my deck. This guy started asking me questions about the different flower starts. He thought I worked there. Turns out he didn't know much about flowers but was doing the same thing as I was. Next thing I knew, we were drinking London Fogs at Starbucks." Anita's face reddened as she finished talking.

Christie grinned. "And did you buy any flowers?"

"Actually, we both did. I helped him plant his selection later that same day."

"So, is this a 'thank-you-for-helping-me' kind of date?"

Anita shrugged. "Well, that was six weeks ago, but he's been busy, so I guess, in a way, he's still thanking me. He's taking me to dinner later this evening at that new restaurant in Sylvania."

"I'll want to hear all about it, girlfriend," said Christie.

"And I want to know more about this wedding. I didn't know anyone with that last name when I lived here before."

Anita had moved to White Castle with her family while in high school, then returned here a few years later after finishing college. Christie and Anita had become friends in high school before Christie also left and spent time in San Francisco being swallowed up in corporate America, and only recently returned to their hometown.

"Me, neither. From what Aunt Doris told me, Conan Starr grew up around Seattle and was transferred here fifteen years ago from somewhere back east to be the big man at the local nuclear plant. His wife, Michelle, is from New York. She hasn't adjusted well to living in a small town and even sent their three kids back east for high school. You know, one of those private boarding schools. I don't know about the two sons, but the daughter, Hailey, whom you just saw, went to Stanford for college and met her fiancé, Ryan Edwards, there."

"If Hailey didn't really grow up in White Castle, I'm surprised she'd want to get married here."

"Apparently, her father insists that he's not paying for a wedding unless she gets married right here in White Castle at the Episcopal church. Michelle explained to me that the groom's mother was pushing for a 'destination' wedding, like in the Caribbean, but Ryan, the groom, wants to make the bride's family happy."

"Smart guy," interjected Anita.

"I get the feeling that Hailey's mother wants to impress Ryan's family with a fabulous wedding, despite this being a small town, and is going all out for a tropical-style look. And I'm going to do my best to make it happen."

"Smart girl," said Anita, giggling. "How can I help?"

The two women spent the next half hour reviewing the flowers that Hailey and her mother had marked, then talking about how to use them to create the right atmosphere.

Christie and Anita had lost track of each other after high school and the ten years following until they both landed back in their hometown.

Christie had been the petite, bouncy, blonde cheerleader who escaped the small town by earning a degree in accounting and landing a job in the big city of her dreams, San Francisco. She had been passed over several times for higher positions—always losing to a male counterpart. By the time Grandma Maude died the year before, Christie had become disillusioned, so when the opportunity arose to be her own boss as florist and owner of the shop where she had worked weekends and summers for her grandmother, she decided to take the plunge.

Anita, on the other hand, was a tall and willowy brunette. Her family had moved to White Castle from Seattle when she was starting high school. She was immediately resented by the girls in her class because all the boys had crushes on her. Over time, she quietly found a way to blend into the local high school culture, primarily through sports and an eye for design. She and Christie bonded through their mutual love of volleyball.

With family money behind her, Anita went out of state to a private university and graduated with a degree in anthropology. When she discovered it wasn't very useful in the marketplace, she went to graduate school for a master's degree in teaching. A few years later, she landed back in White Castle, where she taught English and history at the high school. And had reconnected with Christie when the flower shop reopened the previous fall.

"I love your ideas, Anita. You always did have an eye for creating the best decorations for the high school dances." Christie gave her friend a one-arm hug. "I'll show these sketches to Hailey and her mom when I meet with them in a couple of days."

"You don't have a lot of time to pull this together. Didn't you say you're decorating the country club as well as the church?"

"Yes, but the club has a group of women who will do most of the work there. All I'll have to do is provide the flowers for the tables. Aunt Doris and I will put most of the flowers together here on Friday. Heather will help her finish up on Saturday morning. Then she and Jason will transport them to the club right after we close at noon the next day."

"You got Jason roped into this, too?"

Christie felt her face turn pink. She was still sensitive about the issue of whether or not she and Jason were dating or just old-time friends from high school. "I promised him home-baked cookies if he'd help."

"You know he'd help anyway if you asked, whether or not a bribe was involved." Anita winked at her friend.

"Well, since I need to be doing the fresh flowers at the church in the morning, and Aunt Doris needs to be here, it seemed most logical to let him help get the table decorations to the country club. So I accepted his offer."

"Having an early closing on Saturdays has worked out okay for you, it seems."

"For the most part. I've learned to be flexible on closing time when I know there's a Saturday dance at the school, for example. Then, stay open until all the corsages and boutonnieres have been picked up. Heather, my mom's neighbor girl, has been helping out on some Saturdays as well. And Aunt Doris will almost always cover for me."

The shop came with Aunt Doris, her grandfather's sister, who had worked at the shop for many years and knew practically everyone in town. Having never married and without children of her own, she was everybody's favorite "Aunt," including Christie's. She was Christie's right hand and an invaluable asset at the shop. But Christie greatly valued her friend's help as well.

Christie clarified her working plan. "For the church, we'll put most everything together on-site there Friday. The Episcopal Church has a committee of women who decorate for weddings, and they'll be ready to help when I get there. The flower shipment should be here no later than noon that day. And Father Murphy said I could decorate that afternoon. All we'll have left to do is add the fresh flowers on Saturday morning."

"Sounds like a plan. I'll be free next Saturday to help."

"Thanks, Anita. I hope all the flowers I want will be available. Some of them are unusual but the wholesaler should have them in stock this time of year. I'll call the order in as soon as I hear from Hailey and her mom. Keep your fingers crossed for me. I don't need any bad karma for this event."

CHAPTER 3

*E*arly Friday afternoon, Christie arrived at the church nave with baskets of flowers and big spools of ribbons. She was pleased to find half a dozen women in the front near the altar, chattering with each other while waiting for their assignments. After making preliminary introductions and describing her plan, she demonstrated how to make glamorous bows with long streamers that would grace the tall pillars topped with six-candle candelabras. They were to be placed along the aisles at the end of the pews. Anita would help her tuck fresh flowers in rosy pink and bright salmon colors and add accenting strands of trailing greenery into the candelabras in the morning.

"I need four of you to decorate these pillars while I borrow a couple of ladies to help me with the arch." She pointed to the two women closest to her. "Please take one of these baskets and follow me to the back."

The two young women picked up the designated baskets and followed Christie to the rear of the church, where an arch made of trellis panels had been placed earlier. After seeing one in a magazine, Hailey requested an archway to walk through as she entered the church nave. Christie had been delighted to be able to borrow the arch from the local theatre's prop room. It was already painted a soft green and would be perfect for the flowers that would transform it into the entrance to a garden on a Caribbean island.

She showed the women how to weave the white baby's breath and ivy through the openings in the trellis while she tended to the bright ribbon garlands. She and Anita would create more magic when they added the rest of the fresh flowers the next morning.

Christie chuckled when one of the women asked if there would be a talking parrot as well. "I've heard stories about their language, so, no," she replied. She could only imagine what might happen with a live bird in a church. And all of it bad.

Someone turned on background music with a Caribbean playlist that Christie had brought along. Fingers flew over the next hour while the nave and sanctuary were transformed from their usual "Sunday best" to a lush, pseudo-outdoor setting.

Christie had arranged to borrow pots of shrubs and small trees from a local nursery to add to the effect of a tropical garden. When the delivery van arrived, she directed the placement of the live plants at the sides of the altar, along the sides of the nave, and behind the back pews next to the arch. She hoped the addition of all the greenery would help the guests feel like they were truly in an outdoor venue.

Christie was standing at the back of the church, assessing the overall design, when Michelle Starr walked up from behind her, her face beaming.

"It's magical," she exclaimed, her hands clasped together. "I would never have imagined it could be this beautiful. You really are a magician with plants. Ryan's mother will be impressed."

Christie felt a great sense of relief. She turned and smiled and said a simple, "Thank you."

"THE REST of the flower order arrived an hour ago," Aunt Doris said when Christie walked into the shop a little later. "I sorted the flowers for the church in one tub and the flowers for these table-toppers in another."

Aunt Doris's hands moved quickly as she prepared the shallow, dark-green bowls for the blooms and greenery. Christie had encouraged Hailey to use vibrant colors to perk up the otherwise drab atmosphere of the aging clubhouse and to continue the tropical theme from the church. Ribbon bows in shades of magenta, turquoise blue, rich purple and sunny yellow lay ready on the table to be inserted into the green florist foam after the flowers were placed in position.

Next, Aunt Doris began the task of tucking greens into the large bowls that would grace each of the round tables at the country club reception. Greenery of magnolia and *nagi* leaves with some wispy *plumosus* would "lift" the colorful flowers to elegance while still keeping the total height of the centerpieces low enough to talk over.

Christie sat down on a stool next to the flower cooler with her order on her knee and compared the shipment against her list. The colorful blooms of bird-of-paradise, pink and purple lisianthus, magenta and yellow ranunculus, roses, red ginger, fire opal, and even a few stems of the white hydrangea that Hailey had agreed to lay bundled in the tubs, waiting for their moment to shine. She was puzzled to find a dozen stems of *Amaryllis belladonna* in a deep pink that she hadn't ordered, but the color suited the order, so she figured it was a freebie because she'd ordered so much. She made a mental note to thank the wholesaler.

Heather and Christie began the work of shortening the stems of the flowers that would go into the table-toppers while Aunt

Doris worked her magic creating the final product, adding the flowers, more greenery and the ribbon bows. An hour later, the worktable was covered with the floral creations.

"Those arrangements are absolutely gorgeous, Auntie," said Christie. "We should do weddings more often."

Aunt Doris wiped her hands on the towel on the table. "They're a lot more trouble than doing floral wreaths for a funeral, but it's certainly a happier occasion. And it pays better, I would hope."

"Mrs. Starr didn't blink when I told her what all this would cost. Maybe I should have charged more." Christie winked at her aunt.

"Now, don't go getting all greedy, honey. Word will spread fast if folks think you're just out for the money."

Christie laughed. "If I were in it for the money, I don't think I'd choose a flower shop, but I do love being in charge and on my own."

Aunt Doris opened the door of the flower cooler and retrieved a couple of tubs of flowers. "I'll finish making the bridal party bouquets if you'll help Heather with the corsages and boutonnieres."

"It's a deal," Christie replied. She checked the remaining blooms in the tub. "I think these belladonna flowers will work out in the corsages. I love this bright pink color. The invoice called them 'Naked Lady Surprise Lilies.'" She giggled. "They certainly were that. But why are they called Naked Lady? Do you know, Auntie?"

"It's because they grow on a tall stalk without any leaves, like a bare stalk, or 'naked.' They were probably nicknamed by some guy," Doris said with a scoff.

"That figures. Well, whatever they're called, these are beautiful and will work nicely for the ladies. And if anyone asks me, I'll tell them what they're named and bet it'll make them laugh."

Aunt Doris rolled her eyes. "How about using the crimson

ranunculus as well? That color will coordinate well with the Naked Lady lilies and the pinks and salmon in the bridesmaids' flowers."

Christie nodded, her forehead furrowed in thought. "I like that idea. I also have some lavender calla lilies that will look appropriately exotic for the groom and the groomsmen's boutonnieres. And I'll use the coral ranunculus for the two fathers."

Anita waltzed into the shop shortly before closing time after teaching her final class of the day.

"Can you believe that one of my students named Rembrandt as the first president of the United States?" Anita groaned and tossed her jacket on a chair near the door at the back of the store. "The school year is almost over, and they're supposed to be learning something."

"Is he one of your jokesters?"

"Well, that he is. I was throwing out questions that just might be on the exam next week, and he raised his hand. I thought he was going to ask something about the test, but instead, he started telling me that he'd read something on the internet about how the country was duped into believing that George Washington was the president. And that, in reality, Rembrandt was the man behind the desk."

"Did you remind him that Rembrandt lived a few centuries before 1776?"

"Of course, but he argued that it wasn't *that* Rembrandt. There was another man with the same last name who was President Washington's close advisor."

Christie chuckled. "Oh, my. The glories of trying to teach history when the internet has different versions."

Anita busied herself with making ribbon bows alongside Christie. She picked up one of the deep pink stems and asked,

"What's this gorgeous flower? I don't remember talking about using this one in the decorations."

"That was a freebie from the wholesaler," said Christie. "It's an *amaryllis* that I thought we could use in the corsages."

Anita smiled. "It's a happy color. I'm sure it will be a hit at the wedding."

CHAPTER 4

$\mathcal{C}$hristie hadn't slept well, anxious about finishing the floral touches at the church. She even dreamt about a parrot finding its way into the church and interrupting the sacred ceremony. Grateful to wake up and discover that it was still Saturday morning and nothing bad had happened yet, she threw on her clothes and headed to the shop.

After collecting the tubs of flowers, she hustled to the church, where Anita was already waiting. The two of them wove the flowers and trailing greenery into the candelabra and the archway. Michelle popped in as they were finishing the final touches on the arch.

"Will everything be ready for the photographer in an hour? she asked.

"Yes, Mrs. Starr," Christie replied. "We're just cleaning up after ourselves. Everything is done except for bringing in the parrot."

"Parrot? Did you say 'parrot'?"

Christie giggled. "I was kidding about that."

"But a parrot would fit right in, I think," said Anita.

Michelle scurried off, a funny look on her face.

"I couldn't resist saying that," said Christie, still chuckling. "Hey. We're done. Thanks."

"Are you going to the wedding?" Anita asked. She carried one of the empty tubs to the door.

"I wasn't invited to the ceremony, but I'll look in from the back of the church before I go over to the country club to check on things for the reception."

Anita nodded. "Then I'll see you at the reception. I'll be attending the ceremony with Nathan since he invited me. And he's family."

"THE BRIDE WAS BEAUTIFUL, the flowers were outstanding, and the flower girls were adorable," Anita told Christie that evening when they had a chance to chat at the reception. "The groom's mother was totally impressed that a local flower shop could pull off such a gorgeous wedding. Of course, I had to tell her that you were my friend, and I confess I admitted that I helped a little."

"I am so relieved to hear that she approved! And you helped a *lot*."

Anita grabbed two glasses of bubbly from the waiter as he walked by. "Try this champagne. It's better than the brand I've tasted at The Rock."

Christie laughed. "If they serve champagne there, I wouldn't be expecting the good stuff."

Anita raised her glass. "Congratulations for a job done very well."

Christie took a swallow and nodded appreciatively. "This *is* good. We should order this for our own weddings someday."

The two friends giggled and took another swallow. The sound of loud tapping on a microphone interrupted the loud hum of conversation in the room.

"Welcome, everyone." Conan Starr's voice boomed through

the loudspeakers. "Thank you for being here to celebrate the wedding of my beautiful daughter, Hailey, and my new son-in-law, Ryan Edwards."

The crowd clapped wildly as the young couple stood at the main table and waved. Mr. Starr passed the mic to the best man, Stephen, Ryan's best friend from college, who told a few stories about how Ryan found his soulmate. The best story was about Ryan losing the engagement ring in a poker game and having to win it back the night before he proposed. Then Hailey's friend, Sarah, the maid of honor, shared a litany of adventures, including how the newlyweds had met at a baseball game that they each attended with someone else. They had been sitting next to each other and started talking, and something clicked.

After the toasts were done, the dancing started. Christie noticed one of the young groomsmen and Nathan standing near the punch table. They appeared to be chatting amiably, and by their looks, she assumed they were related. Brothers? Cousins? A couple of middle-aged gentlemen approached them. The older men separated, pairing up with the younger ones. The faces of the younger men quickly changed and suggested anger or maybe disagreement. Curious, Christie sidled up to see if she could hear what they were talking about.

"I suppose your dad there," said the gentleman who now stood by Nathan, directing his words to the groomsman, "would agree with me that there are too many gays in our country. Wouldn't you, Doyle?" He looked at the other older gentleman, took a big swallow of his drink, drained the glass and placed it on the table in front of him. He seemed to purposefully avoid looking at Nathan, who had turned red in the face at his father's words.

The other man said nothing and seemed to shrink under the question.

Nathan raised a hand. "My dad may have an issue, Uncle Doyle, but I personally don't have anything against gays." He turned to the groomsman. "Aaron, I don't believe that people choose to be that way." He put a hand on Aaron's shoulder, but Aaron brushed it off angrily and moved a half step away.

"I can defend myself from your bigot of a father. You're just trying to look good to the family, but you're just like your father: two-faced," said Aaron to Nathan. "And I know you're also sucking up to Uncle Conan and his precious little nuclear plant. I bet you don't find anything wrong even though there have been a whole bunch of complaints."

"And how would you know that, Aaron?" Nathan moved in closer. "What would you know about Omega? What do you even know about *me*?"

"Enough," Aaron replied and turned on his heel.

Nathan threw up his hands and watched his cousin stomp to the table where another young man sat, watching the exchange as had others in the crowd.

"Michelle, I need another glass of Maker's Mark," said Nathan's father to the woman who had come up behind him. "Two ice cubes." He held up two fingers and swayed a little. Christie noted his words were a bit slurred.

"You've had quite enough already, Arthur," said Michelle. "You and Doyle should be ashamed of yourselves. This is a happy occasion, and it's not about you or your issues with Aaron."

Arthur said, "Then I'll go to the bartender and get one myself." He turned with a wobble and headed for the main bar. Doyle headed back to his own table, leaving Michelle to shake her head at the two brothers before returning to her seat.

A few minutes later, Nathan joined Anita and Christie, who were standing on the sidelines. He shook his head.

"I don't understand Aaron at all," he said. "All I was trying to do was compensate for my prejudiced father and explain to his dad that being gay isn't like he has a disease and all that. Aaron got mad at me for trying to defend him. Said he could stand up for himself. Now they're all mad at me."

Anita said, "It'll pass. Let's get some of that cake, and you can tell me more. Christie, why don't you join us?"

Christie shook her blond curls. "I'm not an official guest here, but thanks. I'll hang out by the kitchen until I can start cleaning up."

She watched the crowd that had stayed after the toasts. Some of them were dancing, including the newlyweds and the parents. The men who weren't dancing were hanging out by the bar, refilling their drinks and chatting. She was surprised to observe Aaron approach Nathan and Anita with a couple of drinks in hand, considering the scene she'd witnessed shortly before. Maybe Aaron had cooled off. She imagined it was Aaron being confronted so publicly by his uncle and not defended by his father that had likely triggered him to snap at his cousin Nathan. They exchanged a few words before Aaron left to return to his own table.

By eight o'clock, the crowd had dwindled considerably. Most of the older folks left after a dance or two. The young people were almost all gone except for one young couple on the dance floor. Christie glanced at her watch every few minutes, trying not to be too conspicuous, but she was eager to rescue the reusable decorations and get home. Heather had brought her SUV and was waiting in the parking lot for Christie to give her the signal to come in and get to work. Jason had texted her that he and Doris had already dismantled the wedding decorations at the church and were hauling everything to the shop.

Finally, with only a handful of people in the room, Christie called Heather in from outside and they began the task of transferring the bowls of flowers onto carts to wheel out to the parking lot. Christie was pushing a cart through the doors as Nathan's cousin Aaron came rushing in from outside. "Have you seen Cameron?" he asked her.

"I don't know who that is, but there are still a few people in the room."

He pushed past her, calling, "Cameron! It's time to leave so we don't miss the plane. Hurry up!" He scanned the room, clearly frustrated. He put his hands on his hips. "Cameron! Where are you? Let's go."

"Why don't you check the men's room while Heather and I double-check in these rooms?" Christie suggested to him.

Christie asked her assistant, Heather, to check around the main reception room. "I'll go check the bar while you do that."

A moment later, she heard Heather scream. "Someone needs to call 911! He's not breathing!"

Christie and Aaron appeared simultaneously next to Heather, who was kneeling over a limp, unconscious body lying near the table closest to the outside wall. It was the man who had been sitting at Aaron's table earlier.

"It's Cameron!" Aaron wailed.

A waiter had already whipped out a cell phone and called 911. Christie did a quick assessment of the man, recalling her recent basic CPR training for which she was now appreciative. He had a rapid, thready pulse, a red face and dilated pupils. His breathing was very shallow.

"He's alive," she said. She looked up at the anxious groomsman. "The EMTs will arrive very quickly. I promise. It's a small town."

"Thank you." Aaron took his friend's hand in his own. "He feels cold."

Christie signaled to the waiter to bring a covering, then asked Aaron. "You are...?"

"Aaron. Aaron Starr."

"And..." she looked at the man on the floor.

"Cameron Collins. He's my p— best friend." He wiped tears from his eyes with his sleeve.

The ambulance arrived a few minutes later with sirens blaring. Aaron gave the EMTs basic information about Cameron while Christie stayed out of the way. In a matter of minutes, an IV had been started, an electrocardiogram performed, and Cameron was being wheeled out of the room, Aaron following behind.

Christie and Heather stood together, watching.

"I hope Stormy's hissing at Michelle wasn't a warning that something bad was going to happen," said Heather, who had heard about the latest incident from Aunt Doris while putting the flowers together the day before. When Christie had first opened the shop the previous Halloween, "Stormy," a scrawny black cat, had shown up at the back door. She'd become the shop cat, who occasionally got "hissy." Last time it happened, things had gone south for Christie and her store—something Heather had taken as a sign. Christie didn't want to admit that she had, too, sort of.

Christie put her arm around her young assistant's shoulders. "Let's finish cleaning up so we can each go meet our friends. I'm sure everything will be fine."

CHAPTER 5

J ason met Christie, Anita and Nathan at The Rock after everything was finished up at the country club and delivered to the shop. Anita shared more tidbits of conversation she'd overheard at the reception. Christie admitted she'd been antsy all day, hadn't eaten and was now ravenous. Jason ordered a pitcher of beer to accompany the two pizzas from the wood-fired brick oven. Nathan shared a couple of tales about his relatives and the groom.

"What can you tell me about Aaron?" Christie asked while reaching for a piece of pizza. "I talked with him very briefly at the club after his friend, Cameron Collins, collapsed. From over-hearing an earlier conversation, I assume you and Aaron are cousins?"

Nathan let out a soft whistle. "He's a first cousin. That's one of those things my family doesn't talk about much since he announced he's gay. It doesn't bother me particularly, maybe because I'm younger, but his parents are all bent out of shape over it."

"How do his parents fit into the picture?"

"His dad is one of the three Starr brothers, all of them engineers, all of them straight arrows. My dad is Arthur, the oldest brother; Hailey's dad, Conan, is next in line; and Aaron's dad is Doyle, the youngest."

"That seems quaint," said Christie with an arched brow. "Did your grandparents like mysteries?"

Nathan smiled. "I'm told that my grandmother loved reading books by British authors, but it actually got started when my dad was named after his grandfather, also named Arthur. Naming the other two Conan and Doyle was a natural thing to do, I suppose, for someone who loved Sherlock Holmes."

Christie chuckled. "That's interesting and sounds better than naming them Tom, Dick and Harry. Did you ever wonder what she would have done if she'd had to name a daughter? Anyway, I noticed that Cameron was wearing a boutonniere, but I'm sure he wasn't one of the groomsmen listed on my worksheet. And he wasn't wearing a tux."

"Aaron probably gave him the one he was wearing so he would feel included," said Nathan. "My cousin has a kind heart. My aunt Michelle was pretty upset when she found out that Ryan asked Aaron to be a groomsman in the first place. It got worse when she found out Aaron was planning to bring his partner Cameron as his guest. Of course, Ryan and Hailey are cool about it—that's why they asked Aaron, to keep him included. Younger generation and all, I suppose."

Christie let out a big breath. "That was very sweet of Aaron. I hope Cameron's going to be okay. I hate to think his collapse will spoil any article that might come out about such a great wedding. And one where my flowers were noticed, at that."

Anita patted her friend's arm. "The decorations stand on their own, no matter the circumstances."

"Thanks, Anita. But I'd sure like to know what caused him to collapse. Maybe my mom will find out from her volunteer chums at the hospital."

Nathan's cell chimed, interrupting the conversation. He

looked at the screen. "It's my Uncle Conan." He left the noisy room and went out to the quieter lobby.

Jason asked how things went prior to the incident with Cameron, not having been part of the festivities. Anita and Christie agreed it went smoothly. Then Anita giggled, and Christie smiled, knowing what tickled her. Anita explained to Jason about the flower girls in their coral dresses. "One was about three, and the other maybe four years old. The older one was in front and dropped her petals very carefully, one at a time. The little one was tossing out several at once. When the older one looked back and saw what was going on, she took the little one's basket and tried to demonstrate the 'right' way to do it. Needless to say, the little one tried to take the basket back, and they played tug of war for a moment and dumped all the petals in the middle of the aisle. The little one laughed, and the older one stomped to the front, tears in her eyes. Of course, everyone else was laughing."

"Flower girls always steal the show," said Christie.

"That was Uncle Conan calling about Cameron," said Nathan, returning to the table. "The doctors think he's been poisoned, but not sure with what. He's still unconscious and is on a ventilator, so he isn't able to give any information about what he might have eaten or if he's taken any drugs."

"Poisoned? At a wedding?" Jason asked while shaking his head. "How could that happen?"

"The signs are pointing to something that causes symptoms like atropine, but they won't know anymore until the doctors run the rest of the tests."

"When will that be?" asked Anita.

Nathan reached over and took her hand. "He didn't say when the test results are expected."

"Does your cousin know about this?" Christie asked. "I'd hate for Hailey to have to worry about this kind of thing on her wedding night."

Nathan shook his head. "No. Her mom and dad decided to handle it without telling her. And Cameron isn't a relative, although he is cousin Aaron's partner."

Christie ventured another question. "Nathan, did the emergency room doctor say anything to your uncle about what other things can cause the symptoms that Cameron had? Surely there are a lot of things, like medications."

"Yes, of course," he replied. "Uncle Conan said the doctor named several common meds and asked Aaron to check Cameron's things to see if he was taking anything that could have possibly caused him to collapse. A couple of them were antidepressants that Aaron said Cameron might have been taking."

"I've read about some of the meds we take for the common cold causing weird things to happen to people," said Jason. "I had to do some research a few months ago for a client who was adamant that one of his prescriptions was causing him some side effects. I learned a lot about the topic, including the bit about over-the-counter cold remedies." As an attorney, Jason researched many subjects for client's cases, which Christie found fascinating. Jason was, she had to admit, an intelligent and interesting man.

Christie's thoughts wandered back to Anita, who was saying, "…and sometimes people take two things together that act up, although they're okay one at a time," offered Anita.

"Or they take too much of something, or they drink champagne with a medication that doesn't mix well with alcohol," said Jason.

Anita nodded. "Right, there could be any number of things that result in atropine-type symptoms, even old-fashioned belladonna."

Christie gulped. "Did you say belladonna?"

Jason raised an eyebrow. "Isn't that what they used in the old mysteries, like in Agatha Christie's day?"

Anita nodded. "I've read almost all her books, and it was a popular form of poisoning in that era. But how would he have gotten into anything like that?"

Christie resisted the temptation to reveal that one of her flowers had belladonna in its name. She was certain that the plant wasn't poisonous—at least not unless it had been ingested, and it didn't seem likely any grown-up would eat a bouquet.

The other three went on to talk about a country and western group that would be performing at the historic theatre in Sylvania the following weekend while Christie mulled over the hissing of Stormy, the already shaky reputation of her business, and the flowers she hadn't ordered.

CHAPTER 6

Jason and Anita met Christie at the flower shop after lunch on Sunday to put away the paraphernalia from the wedding and help her get ready for a normal business day on Monday. The empty flower tubs and other decoration items were stacked in the storage room where Heather had stashed them Saturday evening. Jason had picked up the arch from the church and would deliver it to the theatre once all the flowers and foliage were removed. He and Anita busied themselves with that task while Christie took care of the tabletop bowls from the country club reception. The rental company had already picked up the candelabra from the church Saturday evening, and the nursery had just gathered up their rentals, for which Christie was grateful. Two fewer tasks for her to do.

The atmosphere in the shop was heavy with worry on Christie's part, although she knew in her heart that her flowers were innocent in Cameron's situation. She was listening to one of her favorite musicals, *Les Misérables,* on Alexa, but even the music wasn't helping to improve her mood.

"Did your mom learn anything more about Cameron from

her volunteer friends at the hospital?" Anita asked as she tossed wilted flowers, greenery and rumpled ribbon into the trash.

"I didn't ask her yet," Christie confessed. She'd been avoiding bringing up the unfortunate moment despite her intense curiosity. "Did you talk to Nathan today?" She stacked the empty bowls on the counter by the sink and rinsed them out, then left them upside down on a towel to drip dry.

"He tried calling me this morning, but I had my phone in the kitchen while I was grading papers in the dining room and didn't notice till later. He didn't pick up when I called him back." Anita looked over at Christie and added, "What's up, girlfriend? You've been unusually quiet since last night."

Christie sighed. There was no reason not to tell them, and maybe it would help alleviate her concerns. She explained about the mystery flowers and that they were in the belladonna family of plants, a known source of poisoning that was commonly used in old mysteries.

Jason piped up. "Christie, don't worry. It'll turn out to be something that Cameron took before he got to the reception, I'm sure."

"I hope so, but I'm worried about the reaction from people in town. I hope the townspeople don't really believe I have 'killer flowers,' but that incident last fall hurt the shop's reputation for a while. This definitely wouldn't help." Christie's voice wavered.

Anita said with a bounce in her voice, "I bet they'll be talking about the beautiful flowers at the church and the country club instead. Your decorations were exquisite! No one around here has seen anything like what you were able to create. I bet you'll be in demand after this event."

Christie managed a thin smile but didn't share Anita's optimism. "I will admit that it was lovely, though it was quite a challenge to put all that together in such a short time. I have you both to thank for all your help."

"Did you make any money in the end?" Anita asked. "I know some of those flowers had to be expensive. And there were a lot of them." She held up a bedraggled peach-colored ribbon. "Did you want me to save any of these ribbons from the candelabras and arch?"

"I don't have the storage space for the used ribbons, so you can toss them," said Christie. "And, yes, I did make a nice profit. But even so, I wouldn't want to do a wedding like that too often. Aunt Doris might quit on me! She put in a lot of time making the bridal party bouquets and all. Heather was a big help as well. Did I tell you she wants to take a class in flower arranging at the college this summer?"

They all jumped when Anita's phone came to life on the counter, playing a lively hip-hop tune. She picked it up, saying quietly as she pressed the green icon, "It's Nathan," then, "Hi."

The others were all ears, intentional eavesdroppers on Anita's end of the conversation.

"Oh, that's not good…How's Aaron doing?…What? Your uncle said what?…Alright. Is it okay if I tell Christie what you told me? I'm at her shop right now…Okay. Talk to you later. Bye."

Anita's face was grim when she laid the phone on the counter. She looked at Christie and sighed. "Nathan said the police are going to come by to talk to you about your flowers. He said the blood tests came back positive for something like belladonna. The doctors are treating Cameron with everything they've got, but he's just barely hanging on. Aaron is already talking lawsuit if Cameron dies."

Christie's face was ashen. "I swear it's not from my flowers. It can't be. There has to be some other source or a mistake."

Jason reached over and placed a hand on Christie's arm. "Don't worry, Christie. It's too early for anybody to be talking about suing anyone."

Christie's phone vibrated in her back pocket. She saw Chief Conway's name and looked up to the ceiling. They had become acquainted when he investigated a couple of deaths related to a note she'd found in a vintage desk the previous fall. She said softly, "Christie's Flower Shoppe. Hi, Chief."

Anita chewed on her manicured fingernails while she and Jason listened in. Jason clasped his hands together.

"Yes. I'm at the shop…The flowers are here, but some of them are in the trash…Of course…I'll have everything ready when you get here." She ended the call. "My *friend*, Chief Conway, is coming with one of his detectives to collect flowers for testing. He wants one of each to send to the lab."

"On it," replied Anita.

"I'll pull the flowers from the trash," said Jason.

"I'll retrieve the flowers from the tabletop bowls used at the country club," said Christie.

Christie made a copy of the order and the invoice. She laid a towel on the counter for the mangled and wilted flowers that the three of them collected for Conway. Christie checked each one against her list. She had a moment of panic when she realized she didn't see a couple of the blossom types that had been used in the corsages and boutonnieres. She breathed a sigh of relief when she remembered to check the cooler and found a few left-over stems of Naked Lady and ranunculus in a tub.

Conway knocked on the front door a short ten minutes later. Christie unlocked the door and invited him and the detective, Officer McAvoy, to enter. After brief introductions, Conway and McAvoy surveyed the array of flowers. Christie had placed them in the same order as they were on the invoice, with the officers having to trust that she had accurately identified them. McAvoy read the names of each one aloud, stumbling over some of the Latin pronunciations, while Christie pointed to the representative flower. He looked at her with narrowed eyes when he came to the last of the flowers on the invoice. He read aloud, "*Amaryllis belladonna.* Twelve stems."

Anita shot a glance at Christie. Jason looked down at the floor. Christie cringed.

<h1 style="text-align:center">CHAPTER 7</h1>

"Can you explain this in words I would understand?" McAvoy asked with his pen poised to write something in the notebook he'd pulled from his shirt pocket. Conway stood behind him, arms crossed.

"The common name for *Amaryllis belladonna* is Naked Lady," Christie replied. "It's not the same kind of belladonna or nightshade that you read about in old mystery novels. I swear. That variety is *Atropa belladonna* and is much more toxic than the pink flowers here."

McAvoy scribbled a note. "You're sure about that?"

"Yes, of course. And if you look at my order, you'll see that I didn't request them in the first place. They were a bonus, or at least I thought they were at the time."

"How did you use them in your decorations? Could our victim have accidentally ingested any part of them?"

Christie shook her head and pointed to a bright pink flower lying on the towel. She had the unbidden thought that the blooms looked like a lineup in a police station. "I used them in the corsages for the women. I can't imagine how they could have been eaten by anyone."

"I see. The ambulance technician wrote in his notes that Mr. Collins had a boutonniere in his lapel. What flower did you use for that?"

"Well, in the first place, he wasn't on the bridal party list as an usher or groomsman, so he shouldn't have had one at all, but, regardless, it was a calla lily, a very common flower." She pointed to a lavender bloom. "All the groomsmen had the same kind."

"Yes, I was told by his friend, Aaron Starr, that it had been his boutonniere and he gave it to Mr. Collins to wear at the reception." McAvoy scribbled another note and glanced into the flower room. "Did you use any other flowers in the room over there that you might have missed? Maybe something you hadn't ordered but had on hand?"

Christie felt her shoulders tighten with annoyance. She went into the flower room and looked at the stems in the cooler. "No," she answered when she returned, miffed that he asked. And that she hadn't thought of that herself.

McAvoy closed his notebook and re-pocketed it. "That's all for now. If you think of anything else, please give Chief Conway or me a call." He handed her a business card, then rolled up the towel with the flowers inside. "I'll get this towel back to you after I deliver these to the lab for analysis."

McAvoy and Conway walked to the front of the shop and tipped their hats as Christie opened the door. She closed it behind them, locked it, and watched their patrol car until they drove away out of sight before turning to rejoin her friends.

Jason stood and put his arms around her when she reached the table where they had been sitting. "For what it's worth, I know your flowers are innocent."

Christie wiped away a few tears. "I know that too, but I still feel like Conway thinks I'm guilty of something."

"Innocent until proven guilty," quoted Anita. "Which you won't be," she added quickly. "Let's put our heads together and see if we can think of another way that belladonna might have found its way into Cameron."

They sat around the table in the back. Christie poured coffee into mugs, each of which had a different flower motif, and placed a platter of cookies in the center.

"Maybe somebody spiked his drink," suggested Jason.

"I'm sure the police have asked for an analysis of his stomach contents," said Christie. "At least, that's the first thing I would think of."

"I'm going to make a list of the things we come up with so you can give it to Conway," said Anita. "I don't want them to overlook anything."

Jason whistled. "Let's be careful with that. The last thing we want is for them to think we assume they are not competent enough to do a proper investigation."

Christie handed him a couple of pieces of printer paper. "You can write down the ideas."

"I'll work on how to approach them," said Jason, "but for now, let's keep brainstorming. My first question is whether or not someone targeted Cameron. Was there anyone at the wedding or reception who didn't like him?"

"Or didn't approve of his relationship with Aaron?" suggested Christie. "I can certainly see that possibility even in today's climate. Not everyone approves of gay couples being openly gay, especially in a public setting like a wedding."

"We don't know for sure that Cameron and Aaron are gay, do we?" said Anita. "Even if they're best friends."

Jason scoffed. "Anita, come out from under that rock!"

Christie giggled as Anita made a face. "In your defense, my friend, I heard Aaron almost say, 'my partner,' or something like it instead of 'my best friend' when he came rushing in. He acted more like a concerned significant other. And we know from Nathan that Aaron's family wasn't thrilled with the relationship."

"Okay, so let's assume someone might have targeted

Cameron," said Jason. "Who would it have been? How would they have managed to poison him?"

"What does the poisonous belladonna look like?" asked Anita. "Never mind. I'll look it up on Wikipedia. Isn't that where we find the answer to everything?" She picked up her phone and tapped in her question. She sat back in her chair, one leg crossed over the other, reading the screen. Her eyes widened as she sat straight up and said, "Wow. This is something else."

"What are you finding out?" Christie asked.

"Belladonna, or deadly nightshade, is in the same family as tomatoes, potatoes, and eggplant, for one thing." Anita looked up from the screen. "That's a little scary when you think of all the spaghetti sauce and french fries we eat."

She continued, "It's been used since the fourth century B.C. for treatment of wounds, gout and sleeplessness, and as a love potion, if you can imagine. And Cleopatra used extracts of Egyptian henbane, another nightshade, to dilate her pupils."

Jason quipped, "Maybe that's the origin of the phrase 'bedroom eyes.'"

Christie thumped him on the arm before asking, "But how is it used as a poison?"

"I'm getting to that." Anita scrolled through the long passage. "Let's see. It says that all parts of the deadly nightshade plant are poisonous, but the berries are the biggest concern because they're slightly sweet and are especially attractive to children."

"I don't understand why anyone would grow the plant on purpose, especially with children around," said Christie.

"I'd say it's not planted so much as it's naturalized in some parts of the world, including Canada and the United States, according to this," said Anita. "It says here that the berries and seeds are spread by animal droppings and birds. It's not toxic to cattle and rabbits in the wild."

"Good to know. I think," said Christie.

"You still haven't told us how the average person would ingest it," said Jason. "Cameron certainly wouldn't have been eating belladonna berries in a field."

"Well, according to this," Anita continued, "there is one medication available in the United States that contains small amounts of atropine from belladonna alkaloids." She looked at them. "Perhaps you've heard of Donnatal?"

"I remember seeing a prescription bottle of that in Grandma Maude's medicine cabinet," said Christie. "She said she took it for the 'gripes,' whatever that is."

CHAPTER 8

"**I** find it highly unlikely that Cameron would have taken something like that," said Jason after they looked up the definition of gripes, which turned out to be an old name for stomach or intestinal cramps. "In today's age, he would have popped an antacid pill. At least, that's what I'd do."

"Could you ask Nathan if he knows anything about Cameron?" Christie asked Anita. "I mean, like his medical history. Maybe he was the nervous type and had stomach issues."

"I'm not sure they were all that close," replied Anita. "There are definitely some issues among the three families. Nathan told me his aunt Michelle, the bride's mother, was none too happy that Aaron was even invited."

"Why would that be?" Christie asked while getting up to pour more coffee. "He seems like a nice guy to me."

"I agree, but there have been some reports of problems at the nuclear plant where his uncle Conan is the manager, and Nathan was called in to investigate. He hasn't told me anything about what he might have found, but I can imagine it put him in a tough place with the family."

Jason pursed his lips. "I wonder if there was any concern

about Nathan being related to the manager of the plant when he was assigned to check out the complaints."

Anita shook her head. "Nathan told me that he is absolutely bound to investigate without prejudice and is committed to maintaining his integrity. And he was the only agent of the Commission available at the time to manage the issue in a timely manner."

"But if he found anything that puts a bad light on his uncle," said Jason, "it could still cause ill feelings within the family, integrity be damned."

Christie exhaled. "Yes, I can see that."

"But we don't know any such thing right now," said Anita. "We're just guessing."

"I honestly don't care how belladonna, or something like it, got into Cameron's system," said Christie, "as long as the toxicology studies don't find any of it in my flowers."

"You asked if anyone might have targeted Cameron," said Jason. "Let's explore that for a moment."

They were all quiet for a moment. Christie said, "I suppose it could have been someone who was angry about Aaron and Cameron coming as a couple."

"Or someone who didn't like gays in general," offered Jason.

"Or maybe Cameron wasn't the real target," said Anita. "What I mean is that whoever brought the belladonna to the reception, if it was the real thing, maybe intended it for someone else. It could have been truly accidental."

"Poisoning with belladonna is hard to be accidental," said Christie. "And we still don't know that it was actually belladonna that poisoned him. Remember, there are other substances that can cause the same medical situation. Anita, didn't you say that Nathan said that his uncle said..." She sighed, already seeing the problem with figuring this out—too many people and too many unknowns. "...that the blood tests came back positive for something *like* belladonna."

Anita nodded, and they all glanced at each other, the complexity of it all making each pause.

Finally, Christie stood and straightened her shoulders. "Well, too many possibilities, and we don't have enough facts. Besides, it's up to the police to pull all this together. Let's finish cleaning up this mess so we can all go home. We all have real jobs tomorrow. At least, I hope I will still have a business to run."

MONDAY MORNING'S weather was bright and sunny, but Christie felt anything but that. She stumbled through her morning routine with dread. She imagined people calling to cancel orders or not calling to place new ones. She wondered if her aunt had heard the news about the reception. Christie hadn't thought to call to tell her. News traveled fast enough in small towns like White Castle. Especially when it was bad news.

True to form, Aunt Doris was already at the shop, busily putting a birthday bouquet together. Christie lifted Stormy to her official "shop cat" perch above the order desk and unlocked the front door after turning on the rest of the interior lights. She placed a disc of happy music in the CD player and clicked "play."

"Good morning, Aunt Doris," she said in her cheeriest voice. "Did you rest up yesterday?"

Doris looked up from her project. "Yes, but I know *you* didn't, from the looks of everything. Did Anita help you clean up in here, or did you do all this alone?"

"Yes, Anita helped, and Jason, too."

"I heard that the church was beautiful. Mrs. Thompson from the bakery said it was like being at a wedding on a tropical island."

Christie smiled. "I'm glad to hear that our design plan worked."

"Um hmm. Tell me about the reception." Aunt Doris stared at Christie over the top of her half-glasses.

Christie looked up from the order sheet in front of her. "It was very nice, although I only came in toward the end because I was cleaning up at the church with Heather."

"That's not what I mean," said her aunt. "I heard there was an incident. What about that?"

Christie walked back to her aunt's worktable and stood next to it with her hands on top. She chewed her lip. "Some guy collapsed right at the end of the party and was taken to the hospital."

"And is he going to be okay?"

"I sure hope so, Aunt Doris. But it's too early to tell." No other question came up about poison or flowers, even from her aunt, who knew the pulse of the town. Maybe her shop would skate by without repercussions after all.

THE PHONE WAS quiet during the morning, but that was typical for a Monday unless there had been a death over the weekend with a funeral coming up during the week. Christie hoped she wouldn't be getting orders for Cameron's funeral and then realized that even if he died, his funeral would most likely be in his own hometown. She wondered where he was from, which led her to wonder where he and Aaron lived. Maybe Anita knew, or could ask Nathan.

The morning dragged on, broken only by an occasional phone order for someone's birthday or anniversary. She was surprised to see her mother, Maureen O'Mara, enter the shop just before lunchtime. Even though Christie lived and worked in her mother's hometown, she typically only saw her parents when she went to their house for dinner or to pick up something. She'd never had the same close relationship with them as with her Aunt Doris.

"Hi, Mom," said Christie, scooting across the room to give her mother a hug. "What brings you to the store?"

"Well, I was just wondering how you were doing after the excitement at the reception up at the country club Saturday night." Maureen stood in front of the card carousel, perusing the offerings.

"How did you hear about that?"

"One of the other hospital volunteers called me this morning. She was on duty yesterday distributing magazines and heard some people in the family area talking about a possible poisoning at the reception."

"And that brought you here because…?"

"It wasn't exactly your name that was mentioned, but I knew you were the florist for that wedding and reception, so it was easy to figure out." Maureen looked at her daughter.

"Did your friend say anything specific about what the family said?" Christie felt a little nauseated as the conversation progressed.

"That they were angry and seemed to think that the poison came from one of the flowers because of what the police said." Maureen moved on to a table of figurines.

Christie's face paled. "Chief Conway and Detective McAvoy were here yesterday getting flowers to test."

"Oh. I see. Are there any results yet?"

"Not that I've been told, but there were a lot of flowers, and it would probably take a day or two to run all of them through their process." Christie couldn't control the quiver in her voice.

Christie's mom hugged her tearful daughter. "Oh, honey. I'm so sorry you have to go through this. Maybe this is a sign that you should go back to working for someone else?"

Christie straightened her back and stood back. "No way, Mom. I'd rather work for myself, even with days like this. I already tried working for that furniture chain in San Francisco. Ten years under someone else's thumb."

"But you've got your license to be a certified public accountant. Surely, you could work at any real business or even do taxes. Something less risky."

Christie took a big breath. Her shop would never be a 'real business' to her mother. "Nope. Not going to happen. I know my flowers are innocent. I might have to help Conway find the real bad guy because it certainly isn't me."

Maureen hugged her daughter again, although Christie couldn't bring herself to respond in kind. "Your grandma would be proud of you. She had tough skin, too. I'm sure all the locals will be pulling for you. Just wait and see."

Maureen purchased a couple of birthday cards before leaving with a promise from Christie that she'd be at her parents' home for dinner Sunday evening.

"Your mom's right, you know," said Aunt Doris when Christie walked back to help her cut some greenery.

"About what?" she asked defensively.

"Just wait and see. White Castle people stick together."

Christie gave her aunt a genuine hug. At least she always had one member of the family in her corner.

CHAPTER 9

 fter lunch, the shop was busier. Several people called to order flowers for family and friends who had survived cancer.

"Did you know that yesterday was 'National Cancer Survivor's Day'?" Christie asked her aunt.

"No, not until you mentioned it, but that's a good thing to celebrate. How do you know that?"

"The last call was from a lady who works at the cancer center at the hospital. She told me about it and said they want four bouquets for their main desk." Christie handed the order sheet to her aunt. "She said a courier would come by to pick them up about four o'clock today. They're planning a little celebration party for local survivors this evening."

"That's nice. I'll start working on them right away." Doris wiped her hands on her apron, selected four vases, all different, and set them on her worktable. "What about using those flowers left over from the wedding? It would be great to be able to use them for something good. I can fill in with the other stock on hand."

"Great idea, but let's not use any of the Naked Lady. That's just asking for more trouble, I'm afraid," said Christie. "We'll have to use 'breast cancer pink,' of course, for one of the colors. The soft pink carnations will be perfect for that. And teal is for ovarian cancer. I know that because the mother of one of my coworkers in San Francisco had it."

"I think the blue statice will work nicely for teal," said Aunt Doris, reaching into the flower cooler.

The two of them worked side by side to create the arrangements in order to be ready for pickup when the courier arrived, tucking in baby's breath and greenery for fillers. Christie was twirling the last bit of a lavender accent ribbon when the door chime alerted. Instead of a courier, Chief Conway sauntered into the shop. The joy she'd felt while creating beautiful bouquets vanished immediately.

Aunt Doris said quietly, "I can finish these, Christie. You take care of talking with the chief."

Christie took a big breath, wiped her hands on the towel, and managed a small smile as she walked up to meet Conway. "Hi, Chief. Do you have some good news for me?"

Conway tipped his hat and leaned a hip against the order counter. "Not really. But I don't have bad news either."

"What kind of news *do* you have, then?"

"Well, I suppose it's good news that the young poisoning victim is still alive, although he's still in critical condition."

"Does that mean you're here to tell me I'm not under arrest for murder?"

Conway raised an eyebrow and started to open his mouth.

Christie was immediately sorry she'd let that question slip out of her mouth. That was a problem she had—speaking up a bit too quickly. Plus, letting her frustrations show. "I'm so sorry, Chief. I shouldn't have said that. I sincerely hope Cameron recovers, but I hope even more that you find the actual source of the poisoning. Do you have any other leads?"

"Detective McAvoy is working with the doctors at the

hospital on that angle. According to what I'm learning, there are sources other than the plant itself. I was surprised to learn that there's even a prescription medicine called Donnatal that my own mother had in her bathroom. I remembered seeing it when I was looking for a Band-Aid there a few weeks ago."

"That's interesting," said Christie, somewhat relieved. "My grandma Maude had it in her bathroom medicine cabinet, too."

"As you would probably guess," Conway continued, "we're contacting the young man's family to see if he might have been taking it, but they're not exactly close. His friend Aaron, the groomsman, said Cameron's father disowned him when he finally told his family the truth about his being gay. The dad didn't take it well."

"Oh," said Christie. "I'm sure it took a lot of courage to share that information. It's too bad his father had to react that way."

"Yeah. I hope I would be better about it if one of my kids turned out to be gay or one of those other letters."

Christie couldn't hold back a giggle. "You mean the LGBT initials? They stand for lesbian, gay, bisexual and transgender. Sometimes you'll also see the letter Q, for queer."

"Yeah. Those. But it seems like there are more than those when I hear about that stuff in the news."

"There are a lot of different terms thrown around these days, but if you remember the basic four, you're in good company." Christie freshened up the display that was in front of where she and Conway stood.

"Good to know," said Conway. "Now, I have a question for you. Several witnesses from the reception mentioned that Doyle and Arthur Starr appeared to be arguing near the punch bowl. And that you were nearby. Did you overhear any of the conversation?"

Christie sucked in her breath. "Um. I heard Nathan's dad, Arthur, say something to Doyle, that would be Aaron's dad, that sounded like gay-bashing. Nathan stood up for Aaron, but he seemed angry about that. Everyone stomped off mad except Nathan. He looked surprised at Aaron's reaction. That's about it. Why?"

"It occurred to me that Nathan might have been angry enough to poison Cameron," Conway replied.

"What? Are you crazy?" Christie's mouth fell open. "He is the one who defended the idea of Aaron and Cameron as a gay couple. Besides, do you really think he would have conveniently been carrying something that he could use just in case he got the chance?"

Conway said, "Some of the other witnesses don't agree about who seemed the most upset."

Christie gave Conway a look. "Try another idea."

Conway looked at his notes. "Do you know anything about the drinks that the mother of the bride, Michelle Starr, offered a little later?"

"No. Why?"

Conway explained. "Michelle was embarrassed about the ruckus at her daughter's wedding and wanted to make a little peace, so she offered drinks. She said Aaron took a couple of glasses of the spiked punch for himself and Nathan, and Cameron took a non-alcoholic one for himself. He doesn't drink alcohol because of his medication, she was told."

"Oh!" Christie perked up. "So he was on medication. Maybe he was taking something that doesn't mix with alcohol. Is it possible that the glasses got mixed up?"

Conway shook his head. "Don't think so. The glasses of punch served with berries had the alcohol; the ones without berries were plain punch. She said she made it very clear and said that they understood."

"Hmm. Well, I'm glad she tried to smooth things over."

Conway stood up straight again. "Anyway, I just wanted to let you know that the investigation is continuing. We haven't got the toxicology on those plants yet. And I'm not going to throw you in jail. At least, not today."

"You better not, young man," Aunt Doris called from the flower room. "Your mother and I are friends, you know."

LATER THAT EVENING, the doorbell chimed just as Christie finished adding the rum to a pitcher of the fruit juices she'd combined for mai tai cocktails. "Coming," she called from the kitchen.

Stormy joined her at the door, where both Jason and Anita stood on the porch.

"Hey! I'm glad you could come to a meeting of the minds," said Christie as she swooped up her kitty before the cat sneaked out the door in search of a mouse.

Jason quipped, "I would have brought my Sherlock Holmes hat and pipe, but I couldn't find them."

"I brought a plate of cookies," said Anita.

"Perfect," said Christie. "They'll go with your mai tai."

"Fancy," said Jason. "I'm not sure I've ever had one."

The trio settled in at the round dining room table with the coconut macaroon cookies in the center. Christie poured a mai tai cocktail over ice for each of the three. "I searched for a recipe for these online so I could try making them at home."

"This is my new favorite drink," said Anita after tasting the rum concoction. "What made you want to give these a try?"

"I had one a couple of weeks ago when I had lunch with Mom. She insisted I try a taste of hers, and it was yummy, although I don't usually like a sweet drink. I'm pretending we're all in Hawaii." She raised her glass. "Cheers!"

"And the coconut cookies are perfect for an imaginary visit to Maui," added Jason. "This cocktail is pretty good, even if it's not usually a guy's drink."

"Well, Jason—I don't have any scotch, so you'll just have to drink your mai tai." Christie made a face at him. "Anyway, I asked you two to come over to help me come up with some plausible scenarios for Chief Conway to consider for finding the source of the belladonna."

"You don't really think he believes you could be guilty, do you?" Anita asked with her brow furrowed.

"No, but somebody is, and he or she should be held accountable, especially if Cameron dies. Conway said he's still in critical condition but holding his own. But with Conway coming by to update me and all, well, I think he'd be okay with us helping to at least come up with ideas. He mentioned Nathan as a suspect as well, by the way."

"Nathan?" Anita scoffed. "No way."

"Conway mentioned that he had interviewed witnesses to the angry verbal exchange between Aaron and Cameron at the punch bowl. He wondered if Nathan was angry enough to try to poison Cameron in revenge, but I reminded him that he would have to be carrying the poison with him at the time."

"Seems unlikely," said Jason. "So we're back to asking ourselves whether the poisoning was intentional versus accidental. And if intentional, who was the perpetrator?" He looked at Christie, then Anita.

"And was the poison meant for Cameron or someone else?" added Christie.

"And how did the poison get into Cameron? Surely, he didn't eat anything that nobody else ate at the reception," said Anita. She held up her glass. "I'm liking this mai tai. Please don't tell me how many calories are in one of these!"

"I won't," said Christie, "but I'm sure you burn enough calories with your busy day to cover your drink."

"I wonder if the focus is on belladonna just because it's the name of one of your flowers," said Jason. "There have to be other possible sources that the doctors and Conway should consider."

"I'm looking it up again," said Anita. "Here's the answer, according to Wikipedia. It says that the belladonna from deadly nightshade doesn't show up in blood tests, although it can show up in the stomach if it's been ingested within the previous hour or so."

"Conway didn't say if they found anything in Cameron's stomach or if they pumped it at all," said Christie. "Go on."

"Then it lists quite a few medications that can cause a similar reaction, such as antidepressants and scopolamine for motion sickness and atropine for nerve gas poisoning. There's even the possibility of it occurring after taking too much Benadryl, like in an overdose attempt."

Christie groaned. "Gee. Cameron could be depressed and taking one of those antidepressants, and if he added an antihistamine for a cold, it might have been too much for his system."

Jason reached over and grabbed another cookie. "It's not our job to figure it out. The doctors should be getting a history that would rule out some of those possibilities."

"Except that with him being unconscious, it's impossible to get definitive answers to those questions," said Christie. "Aaron may not even know all of the answers." She leaned back in her chair and took a big swallow of her drink.

"Conway also has to consider whether or not Aaron is telling them the whole story, or the truthful story," said Jason. "For example, what if Aaron or Cameron has something to hide? Maybe they are into marijuana or something else not legal everywhere that they might have taken to brace themselves for this wedding, and that doesn't mix with a medication?"

"I think I'm getting a headache," said Christie.

"Christie," said Jason, "you said something about Cameron maybe not being the intended victim. I wonder if there's someone else in the wedding party who was meant to partake of whatever the poison was."

"*If* it was a poison," said Anita. "We just listed a whole bunch of other possibilities."

Christie sat up straighter. "Anita, remember when we were chatting when Hailey and her mother were at the shop picking flowers, and Nathan's name came up? Hailey's mom, Michelle, overheard us and definitely had an icy tone when she stated Nathan was her nephew."

"Yes!" said Anita. "And Stormy jumped down and hissed. And she commented that the cat didn't like the mention of Nathan's name either."

Christie said thoughtfully, "Maybe Stormy was hissing at Michelle instead of the word 'Nathan.'"

Everyone was silent.

CHAPTER 10

uesday morning, Christie sat on the stool at her order station, elbow on the counter, pen poised to write.

"Are you done with that order, Honey?" Aunt Doris called from the flower room, where she was busy making a floral arrangement for a grieving widow.

"Just about. How many *alstroemeria* do you think I should add to the list? We used everything we had for the wedding."

"I can use them for almost anything, so you should definitely ask for two dozen stems. Be sure they give us two or three different colors."

"Okay. That coral was gorgeous if they still have some of that."

"That would be good," replied her aunt. "Bright pink or a deep yellow are also great colors to work with."

"Got it."

Christie hit the "submit" button, then turned her attention back to the notes from the discussion she'd had with Jason and Anita the previous evening. She mulled over the possibility that Michelle Starr was upset enough about Nathan that she'd try to poison him. And somehow inadvertently caused Cameron's illness instead? She couldn't bring herself to think it was likely. While she realized it wasn't impossible for a woman to be capable of such a devious move, she couldn't convince herself that Michelle had a good enough reason to be offended by either Nathan or by Aaron and Cameron's relationship. If Aaron had been her son instead of a nephew, maybe. But why call attention to the situation at a wedding? Surely there were better opportunities, like a family picnic.

The front door chimed, and Christie looked up to see Michelle waltz in. She was dressed to the nines in a navy blue sheath that fit her trim figure well, accompanied by a sassy cloche on her head, ecru heels, and a Michael Kors handbag. She was not smiling.

"Good morning, Mrs. Starr. How can I help you?"

"I came in to ask about a discount for the flowers at the reception."

"I don't offer discounts after the fact. What would be the reason?" Christie's stomach churned. Her heart raced. She hoped Cameron was still alive and would recover.

Michelle stood in front of Christie's desk. "You certainly must realize that one of my wedding guests, Cameron, is ill because of your flowers."

Christie willed herself not to speak her true mind. Not easy to do. "I'm sorry? Do you mean to say that Cameron *ate* the flowers?"

Michelle's face reddened, and her facial features sharpened. "Isn't it obvious to you that it has to be your flowers that caused him to get sick?"

Christie calmed herself. "I'm quite sure we shouldn't be having this conversation, Mrs. Starr. The police are still investigating to find the source of what made Cameron ill. And if it were the flowers, I would expect many more people to have become ill." *Unless he ate them,* she thought to herself.

Michelle straightened her shoulders and stepped back from the counter. "I would think you would want to keep your reputation from being tainted when people find out you used poisonous flowers."

"Which I didn't do, of course." Christie gritted her teeth. "The lab results will be back soon, I'm sure."

Michelle huffed and turned around stiffly. She said over her shoulder as she walked toward the door, "You might reconsider giving me a break on those flowers."

Christie watched her walk out the door and to her car before standing up herself. She was shaking and didn't trust herself to walk on her wobbly legs. Aunt Doris approached her from the flower room, where she had been all ears.

"Don't worry, Christie," she said with her hand on her niece's shoulder. "We all know she's upset and wants to be able to blame somebody or something. Conway will take care of things."

Christie wiped away a tear with the sleeve of her shirt. "I know you have confidence in me. But I'm not sure about Conway. What if the lab tests show something? What if the Naked Lady flowers were somehow the source of belladonna, even though Cameron didn't eat them?"

"Now, now, Honey. How many years have I been back here putting flowers together? How many bouquets have had a Naked Lady flower in them without anyone getting sick? It will all work out. You'll see." Doris hugged her niece and said, "Let's get these tabletop arrangements ready for the ladies from the White Castle PTA. Mrs. Campbell said she'd pick them up at eleven, and it's already ten thirty."

Christie sighed and followed her aunt to the flower room. "I don't like Mrs. Starr very much."

"You'll probably never see her again, so don't spend another minute wasting your energy on her. But I hope you cashed the check already."

Christie managed a small chuckle. "It's in the bank and already accounted for." Then her smile faded. "Unless it bounces. Or she stops payment."

CHAPTER 11

Sheila Campbell showed up promptly at eleven to lay claim to the half-dozen tabletop arrangements. "These are beautiful," she exclaimed. "We're planning to raffle them off at the end of the meeting. It's a small way to raise a little more money that will go into our scholarship fund for the outstanding seniors each school year."

Christie tallied the order and handed the receipt to her customer after running the credit card. "That's a lovely idea. I hope you make a lot of money doing that."

"Everyone's excited about seeing what your flowers look like after the big wedding last Saturday," said Sheila, smiling broadly. "You're the talk of the town."

Christie hesitated to say anything other than thank you, not certain she wanted to hear what the "talk" was. Would it be the reception decorations? Or Cameron's collapse?

"The ladies at St. James Episcopal said it was the most beautiful wedding ever!" Sheila gushed. "It almost makes me wish someone in my family were getting married soon. But my daughter's only in the eighth grade."

Christie smiled. "You'll have to wait a while, I think. Thank you for the nice comments. And have a great raffle."

Aunt Doris had come up to Christie's desk during the conversation. "I told you there was nothing to worry about," she said with a hand on her niece's shoulder.

Jason came into the shop a few minutes later. He held a copy of the morning newspaper from the bigger city, Herald Falls, which was twenty miles up the freeway. He handed it to Christie. "Take a look at the lead article."

Christie unfolded the paper. The headline was in a bigger font than usual and read Nuclear Plant Under Investigation. Christie and her aunt stood side by side, scanning the article that covered more than half of the front page above the fold.

"This doesn't look good for Mr. Starr," said Christie. "Hailey's father, I mean, now that I know there are a bunch of Starr brothers."

"Yeah." Jason let out a soft whistle. "I'll bet the family tension has skyrocketed between Nathan and his uncle Conan, being as he's in charge of the nuclear plant across the river."

Christie cringed. "Timing's not the best."

"But it might take some heat off you," said Aunt Doris.

"And put it right on Conan Starr," replied Christie. "Michelle might have seen the paper before she came in earlier today. Maybe that's why she was so hot under the collar."

"Mrs. Starr was in here today? Why?" Jason asked.

Christie raised a shoulder. "She was hinting—essentially demanding—that I give her a discount on the flowers because of the incident at the reception."

Jason scoffed. "She can't possibly think your flowers were actually the cause of Cameron's getting sick. Can she?"

"I think she wants to push me around a little and bully me into giving her a better deal. Maybe I should have charged more, after all."

"Christie!" said Aunt Doris from her workroom. "You can't

charge Seattle prices in a little town like this. You did the right thing, and she still got a bargain compared to those bigger shops."

"I'm just venting, Auntie. I don't want to price myself out of the market. Not that there will be a lot of weddings around here, anyway." Christie missed the look that passed between Jason and her aunt.

"I don't suppose you've talked to Anita today, have you?" asked Jason. "She might know more about this whole deal."

Christie shook her golden curls. "She'll be busy with students till school's out at three. And I doubt that she and Nathan would discuss the nuclear plant. Whatever he's uncovered would have to be confidential information, I would think."

"Yeah," replied Jason. "He strikes me as an upright kind of guy who wouldn't be sharing information inappropriately." He glanced at his watch. "Gotta run. You can keep the paper. I bought it for you because I know you don't subscribe yourself. I'll call you later if I find out anything else."

"Hey, thanks," said Christie. "Ciao."

"Bye—to you, too, Aunt Doris." Jason turned back to wave as he exited the front door.

"He's a nice young man," said Aunt Doris. "I'm glad you guys are dating."

Christie felt her face redden. "We're not dating. We're just friends."

"So you say," replied her aunt, as she walked back to her worktable. "Might be the same thing."

Christie rolled her eyes with her back to her aunt and checked the latest emails. She was surprised by how many solicitations and offers she received for credit cards, accounting assistance, and other typical business services. She reminded herself that the e-bots didn't know she had a degree in accounting and was quite capable of managing on her own.

Her aunt picked up the phone when it rang a moment later, as she usually did because most of the calls were for orders, fortunately, and Aunt Doris was still better at taking care of that end of business. For now, anyway.

"It's for you, Christie. Line one."

Christie halfway expected it to be Chief Conway or Anita but was thrilled to hear a different, familiar voice instead.

"Missy! It's nice to hear from you. What's going on?"

"I couldn't wait to tell you the news. I was worried you'd hear it from someone else, so I decided to call because I wanted you to hear it from me first."

"What news?" Christie asked, a shiver of dread running through her body with Missy's use of the word "worried."

"Brian proposed! And we're getting married in September."

"Oh, Missy. That's wonderful! Tell me more!"

"We haven't decided on everything, but we know that you will be doing the flowers and my brother, Father Timothy, is going to preside over the ceremony. It was you and my brother, after all, who managed to get us back together."

"I'd love to do the flowers. I'll even give you a 'friends and family' discount." Christie giggled.

"No need to do that, but thank you for the offer."

"Will the wedding be held in Olympia, where you live now?"

"Actually, no. We talked quite a bit and decided to get married in White Castle. That's where we met and fell in love. And it feels right to continue our story there, where we left off."

"That's a sweet reason. What about your parents? Have they come around to accepting Brian?"

"Yes, thanks to my brother," said Missy. "And to you for discovering the truth about that terrible night forty years ago."

"If it hadn't been for the note I found in that old desk," said Christie, "we still wouldn't know the truth."

"Brian and I are both glad the right guy is in jail this time. Anyway, I'll come down to White Castle soon and give you more information. Oh...I should tell you the date. We have to coordinate with my brother because of his parish schedule, so it's going to be Saturday, September fourteenth. Will you be free that day?"

Christie chuckled. "I don't even have to look at a calendar to know that your wedding will be the only event on my schedule that day. Consider it done."

After ending the call, Christie held the phone in her hand for a moment, smiling, before replacing the handset. She had met Missy and Brian the previous autumn while tracing the origin of a cryptic note she'd found in the shop while setting up for her grand opening.

"Aunt Doris. We're going to do another wedding."

CHAPTER 12

Tuesday evenings were quiet for Christie. She and Stormy typically curled up in her grandma's reclaimed chair with Christie reading a book, often a mystery, or researching new ideas for floral arrangements. Still a newcomer to being an owner in the flower business, she had quickly learned that she had to keep up with the latest trends in colors, styles of bouquets, and even the most popular blooms. This was unlike her previous stint in the furniture world, where styles changed slowly. She realized that flowers were like the hare and furniture was like the tortoise in the sense of the children's classic story.

She was enthused about creating a romantic floral backdrop for Missy and Brian's wedding in the fall. The Catholic church would be a beautiful setting and lent itself to using pillars topped with candelabra and flowers spilling down the sides. Light would be streaming through the leaded glass windows and onto the happy couple at the altar. When thoughts about Cameron's mysterious illness and the possible connection to the decorations she'd prepared for the Starr-Edwards wedding crossed her mind, she felt a moment of gloom but shook it off. She was sure of her own innocence and remained cautiously optimistic that she would still be in business at the time of Missy's wedding.

Jason called while she was sketching a design for the altar. In addition to the pillars on each side of the bride and groom, she pictured several large bouquets. They would be beautiful in any color combination that Missy chose and could be used the next day for the church service. Christie liked creating arrangements that could be used for more than one occasion.

"You'll never guess who called today," she said dramatically after the usual pleasantries.

"Does that mean I shouldn't even try?"

"You have to try at least a couple of guesses, or I won't tell you."

Jason groaned. "Your mother."

"Of course not. That's not even a valid guess."

"Chief Conway?"

"That's a better guess, but not him either." Christie pictured Jason squirming in his chair.

"You already told me I'd never guess, so just tell me. You *know* you want to."

"It's Missy."

"You mean the Missy from that letter in the desk?"

"Yes. She called to tell me that she and Brian are getting married in September. And she wants me to do her flowers."

"That's awesome. But doesn't she live in Olympia? How will you manage doing the flowers up there from White Castle?"

"Easy. She's planning to get married here in town at St. Thomas Catholic Church. She said her brother, Father Timothy, is going to do the honors."

"That's great, Christie. I'm glad for the happy ending to that story."

"You and me both," Christie sighed romantically, recalling how she found the mystery note addressed to Missy in that desk and reunited it with the young woman herself. Which led to

Missy meeting Brian, and, well, Christie sighed again…so glad things worked out. Suddenly aware she had Jason still hanging on the phone, she asked, "What kind of news do you have? You said you were going to call me this evening if you found out anything else, which must mean you know something."

"My secretary, Kenna, told me she'd heard some stuff about the nuclear plant investigation."

"How would she find out anything?"

"Turns out she's good friends with Michelle Starr," Jason replied.

"I see. And Michelle's husband is the manager at the nuclear plant. What did she say? Can you tell me?"

"She didn't have any actual facts, but this is apparently the second time something has happened that triggered an in-depth investigation by the Nuclear Regulatory Commission, according to what Michelle told her."

Christie said, "Hm. I'd never heard of that agency until Anita said Nathan worked there. I thought the Atomic Energy Commission was in charge of monitoring nuclear plants."

"That's ancient history, Christie. The Atomic Energy Commission was abolished in 1974 by the U.S. Congress."

"Way before my time," Christie said with a giggle. "No wonder I don't know about it."

"Anyway, the regulatory programs of the AEC came under strong attack years ago after some major safety incidents. So, Congress created a new law and disbanded it. Then they created two new agencies: the Energy Research and Development Administration and the Nuclear Regulatory Commission, which is the one that Nathan works for."

"More than I needed to know, but so what?" Christie added additional detail to her wedding sketch with colored pencils.

"Well," said Nathan, "this particular plant apparently has been in the crosshairs of the regulators before for reported safety concerns. Kenna said Conan Starr has been worried about getting shut down and thinks someone at the plant might be setting him up."

"Ooh. That doesn't sound good. No wonder she's a little testy about Nathan."

"Understandable, to a degree," said Jason. "From what I understand, Nathan is here to determine whether or not there's anything to the recent complaints."

"Does he know anything yet?"

"According to what Michelle told Kenna, Nathan has requested report after report. She thinks he's on a witch hunt to get her husband."

"But wouldn't that be standard practice to get to the bottom of things?" Christie asked. "I mean, it's awkward that Nathan is the nephew of the plant manager, but I would guess he's pledged to practice impartiality."

"It is awkward, and, yes, he would be required to uphold the same standards for any investigation."

"Well, I'm sure Nathan isn't expecting any invitations to his aunt and uncle's house for Sunday dinner." Christie finished her sketch and set it aside.

"Speaking of dinner, do you want to get together with Nathan and Anita for dinner on Friday night? There's a decent movie at the theater that we could see afterward. "

"Sounds great. I'll let you set it up with Nathan."

"Will do. Let me know if you hear from the chief. Okay?"

"Of course. You'll be my first call. Thanks for calling, Jason. Ciao!"

As Christie ended the call, she hoped she wouldn't need to call an attorney after her next conversation with Chief Conway, whenever it occurred.

CHAPTER 13

As it was, she didn't have more than a minute to even think about that possibility because Anita called next.

"You must have ESP," said Christie. "I was just talking to Jason about Nathan and his uncle Conan."

Anita laughed. "If I had ESP, I'd be able to figure out what these students of mine are thinking when they write these English essays. So why were you two talking about Nathan?"

Christie briefed Anita on what Jason had learned from his secretary.

"It surprises me that Jason would share what sounds like gossip."

"I guess I didn't think of it like that. He thought I would want to know the scuttlebutt before I heard it from someone else."

"Or he just wanted a reason to call you," Anita said playfully.

"Have you talked to Nathan today?" Christie changed the subject.

"No, and I wouldn't expect to with me at school and him at the plant. Why?"

"I was just wondering if he's said anything to you about what's reported in the paper."

"Umm. We haven't talked about his work much. He's quite discreet about that."

"Good to know," said Christie. "Do you have any idea about how long he's going to be here? Planting flowers seems like something you do when you're planning to stay in one place for a while."

"They were simply patio pots. Nothing permanent about those," said Anita. "He hasn't said anything about future plans, but he did say he usually works out of his office near Dallas, Texas, and he doesn't typically do this kind of fieldwork anymore. He's filling in for an investigator who has been reassigned to in-house work because he's undergoing chemotherapy and has a weak immune system. The complaint that came in needed to be handled promptly, and Nathan knows the job because he had done investigative work earlier in his career. He said that's why he got selected, even though he tried to decline."

"Because his uncle is the manager at the plant?"

"Yes," said Anita. "But it's supposed to be a quick in-and-out field job limited to checking out a complaint. He says these come in all the time, and there's usually nothing to them, so he didn't anticipate finding anything significant. But the NRC has to treat each one seriously because the public is still generally wary of nuclear power."

"Then why is his aunt Michelle acting like Nathan is out to get his uncle?" asked Christie.

"Nathan says there's been acrimony between Conan and Arthur, his father, forever, going back to high school days when they played football and baseball and fought over some of the girls." Anita laughed. "Anyway, Nathan walks on eggshells around Conan all the time, he says, whether it's family stuff or work."

"I can see how he'd like to avoid getting into a war with the family over this."

~

CHRISTIE sipped on her glass of wine, a nice crisp pinot grigio that was perfect for the summer-like weather, and mulled over what she'd learned from Jason and Anita. The tension that Conan Starr felt at the nuclear plant seemed to spill over to his wife, as seemed logical. Nathan's presence in the community related to his job had to be another factor in the chilly relationship among the various Starr family members.

Stormy stirred in her lap, purring contentedly. Christie idly scratched her kitty behind its black ears.

"What do you have to say about this, Stormy?" She tried to recall everything she'd heard at the reception. Aaron said something about 'missing the plane' when he was looking for Cameron. That led to her realizing that she didn't know where they lived, nor would she normally have had any reason to care about that. That thought led her to wonder what kind of work Aaron and Cameron did in their normal lives. And if Cameron was going to be able to return to a normal life. That sparked the idea to call her mom.

"Christie! How nice to hear from you," said her mom. "Is everything all right?"

It was unnerving that her mom always seemed to know when something was awry, even before Christie had said anything more than, "Hi, Mom." She shivered. "I guess so. I have a wedding scheduled for September, and we're still getting orders for birthday bouquets and anniversaries, so that's all good."

"A wedding? Marvelous!" Maureen's tone changed. "But there's obviously something that's not good. What is it?"

Christie sighed. She didn't want to burden her mom with her own worries but needed to ask her about Cameron, so she plunged ahead. "I haven't heard anything about Cameron Collins today—you know, the young man who collapsed at the Starr-Edwards wedding. Is there any new scuttlebutt at the hospital?"

"Honey, you know that as a volunteer, I don't hear anything but a little gossip about patients, and usually, I don't know who it is."

"I know that, but can you tell me anything?"

Christie heard her mother exhale loudly before she talked.

"This isn't against HIPAA, I suppose," Maureen said. "I mean, it has nothing to do with a medical condition, but I heard that the police were at the emergency room again. They were asking about the clothing that came in with Collins."

"What about it?"

"One of the volunteers said she'd heard that a jacket got lost, and the family is all agitated about it. Even the head of risk management is getting involved, I guess to try to avoid a lawsuit over it."

"A lawsuit over a lost jacket? Really?" Christie conjured up an image of the sharp-looking sports coat Cameron was wearing when he was found.

"Yes. Really."

"Did they find it?"

"I don't think so. At least, not that I've heard. I sure hope someone finds it before too long. No need for more drama with that family."

"So do I," said Christie, commiserating. "I wonder what's so important about the jacket. It was just a standard blazer that he was wearing when I saw him lying on the floor."

"I did hear something else," her mom continued, "but it wasn't about the jacket. Deb, who works at the bookstore, said they're having a run on murder mystery books that include death by poison."

"What? Why would that happen?"

"I didn't see it, but she said one of their customers brought in an article from the Herald Falls paper from yesterday. There was a story in the society news about the big wedding and the collapse at the reception. The reporter had been there to cover the wedding at the request of Michelle Starr."

"Oh, no," Christie groaned. "I don't need any more bad news."

"Oh, Honey, I gotta go. I've got an apple pie in the oven, and I hear the timer buzzing in the kitchen. I'll let you know if I hear anything more. Okay? Love you, dear. Thanks for calling. Bye."

"Love you, too, Mom. Later."

Christie took a sip of her wine, which was no longer as cold as she liked. "What could possibly be so important about that jacket?" she asked Stormy as she fired up her laptop and searched for the society news section from the day before. She found the reporter's name and contact information and dialed.

Madison Lewis sounded as young on the phone as her first name suggested. It had been a trendy name some twenty years earlier, Christie recalled.

"Yes, I was at the wedding and the reception," she acknowledged. "Mrs. Starr wanted to be sure her daughter's wedding got the proper attention."

"Surely you don't think the flowers were the real cause of the problem, so why did you imply that they were in your article?" Christie felt her face burn.

"I didn't say anything like that. I just listed the names of the flowers that I got from looking them up on the internet. Did you know that there's an app that gives you the name when you take a picture with your cell phone? And one of them was belladonna. Just like the information that Mrs. Starr got from Aaron and shared with me. Of course, you already knew that because they were your flowers," Madison said smugly.

"Did you see anyone eat any of those flowers?"

"Of course not, but I wasn't there the whole time. I let the readers come to their own conclusions. I just report facts."

"I believe you made an inaccurate assumption that the flowers caused the collapse of the young gentleman. The fact is that the particular flower I used is not related to—"

"Listen. I saw the ambulance myself. I'm just a reporter. Not an analyst. The flowers were beautiful, by the way. Have a good day."

Christie heard a dial tone. She made a face at the phone and groaned.

CHAPTER 14

*L*ate spring flowers were in full bloom in the neighbors' yards as Christie drove the mile or so to her flower shop Wednesday morning. She loved seeing the Japanese maples unfurl their narrow, fringed leaves and the buds opening up on the peonies and azaleas. The tulips and daffodils had already had their show of spring blooms a few weeks earlier, making way for the newest blaze of color.

The city park that she passed on her way was brilliant in all shades of green. The deciduous trees had finally "redressed" themselves with their leaves. In her free time, she never tired of taking leisurely walks along the lake bank and took pride in being able to name most of the trees as she strolled by. She recognized American oak, dogwood trees in both pink and white, California redwood, sugar maple, and several varieties of Japanese maple, to name a few.

The park had been created by the city founders, who had set aside a beautiful piece of land around a small lake near the town's center. It was a lovely place for picnics, weddings, walking or running, or just relaxing with a book under a tree.

Today, she saw only a handful of walkers—some with their dogs —and a group of children walking with a teacher near the elementary school. Maybe working off some restless energy, she thought, with the school year ending soon.

Aunt Doris greeted her as soon as she and Stormy entered through the back door. She said quietly, standing with her back to the front entrance. "Chief Conway has been waiting for you. He wants to ask you some more questions about that belladonna flower we used in the corsages."

Christie squared her shoulders after she hung up her windbreaker and lifted her cat to its shelf above the main counter. She walked to the front door, opened it, and motioned to Conway, who was sitting in his cruiser in front of her store.

"Good morning, Chief. Come on in. Aunt Doris tells me you have some more questions."

Her aunt had steeped some tea and offered some to the chief and Christie.

"Why, that's very nice of you," he said as he accepted the mug with Christie's new shop logo. He sat on the stool next to the main counter and stretched out his long legs.

"I'm ready," said Christie. She stood at the counter facing the chief, leaning on her elbows, hands clasped.

"The lab wants to know more about this one plant—the one that ends with the word belladonna. What can you tell me about it?" He had his pen poised to take notes.

Christie quickly pulled up information from her laptop and let the chief read it for himself.

"How can you be sure this flower didn't cause the problems that the young man suffered? Why did you use it in the first place?"

Christie explained the difference between the two plants, *Amaryllis belladonna* and *Atropa belladonna,* the same facts she'd wanted to tell that reporter who had no interest in facts at all. "The first version, the amaryllis, is very common and is planted in people's gardens everywhere. Maybe you've seen the tall plants with huge blooms that are often given as gifts at Christmas time. They come in a small flowerpot, and you water them and wait till they bloom about six weeks later." She went on to point out the text that explained *Atropa belladonna* was commonly referred to as deadly nightshade and was, in fact, quite toxic, affecting the central nervous system, causing disorientation, coma and death. On the other hand, *Amaryllis belladonna,* though toxic when taken internally, normally only causes abdominal issues. She explained, "The word 'belladonna' simply means 'beautiful woman' and happened to be included in the name for both plants."

After a couple of minutes of reading, Conway asked, "Are you sure about the plant that came from your wholesaler? I know the invoice described it as a belladonna plant, but how can you be sure it wasn't the bad one, the one called 'nightshade'?"

She showed him photos of the two groups of plants. "You can see that they don't look anything alike." The deadly nightshade's small, purple, bell-shaped flowers were nearly inconsequential compared to the trumpet-shaped bloom of the safe belladonna plant.

Aunt Doris joined them from her usual station at the flower worktable. "And because I've been working with flowers for fifty years. *That's* how." She wiped her hands on her apron, which was stained with too many shades of green to count. "You better be looking for some other way that the young man got sick because it wasn't from any flowers that came from this store. And don't you be saying otherwise."

Conway exhaled noisily. "Yes, Doris. We are looking for a source, any source, but I had to ask the question because of the name of the flower."

"Are you looking at any other suspects?" Doris pointed her index finger at the chief. "There were a lot of people at that wedding and the reception. What about considering one of them?"

"Yes, Doris. I got the guest list from Michelle Starr. The detective is busy interviewing them."

"Humph." Doris stomped back to her flowers.

Christie stood a little straighter, proud of her aunt standing up for her and her flowers. An awkward silence was broken when Christie asked, "How is Cameron doing, Chief, if I may ask?"

"He's still in critical condition, but I understand the doctors think he's going to survive. We can't ask him any questions yet. Maybe in a couple of days, he'll be off the ventilator and the heavy sedation and can tell us something."

"That's a relief," said Christie. "I'm sure you're looking into all the possibilities, but my friends and I were talking about this a couple of days ago, and we found a lot of ways that people can end up with this kind of condition, other than from the nasty belladonna plant."

"Yes," said Conway, nodding. "The doctors are talking with the family members and searching for other explanations as well. That's all I know at this point."

"Okay. Thank you for sharing that. I'm feeling relieved knowing there are other people you are looking into."

"Fortunately, we operate under the principle that people are innocent until proven guilty in a court of law," said Conway.

Christie nodded. "But there are those who jump to conclusions regardless of a lack of evidence."

Stormy used that moment to jump down from her perch and sat in front of the chief, staring at him.

Conway backed away from his stool and said, "Is your cat trying to tell me something?"

Christie said stiffly. "Maybe she's telling you to try harder to find the guilty person." She picked up Stormy, who purred in her arms.

Conway pocketed his notebook and pen. "Well, Christie. And

Doris. Thank you for your time. We'll keep looking. And at least for now, we're not looking for a murderer. Just a poisoner."

Christie accompanied the chief to the front door. Walking back to her desk, she felt her heart thud, and a chill ran down her spine. She didn't feel very relieved by Conway's last comment. Could he really still think she might be a poisoner?

CHAPTER 15

$\mathcal{C}$hristie shared the society news article from the Herald Falls paper while she and her aunt created an arrangement in the Japanese ikebana style that was to be used on the head table at an event at the local community college.

"I don't think there's much you can do about that article," said her aunt, empathizing with Christie's angst. "And really, how much society news does the average person read these days?"

Christie shrugged. "It's unfair that people can write anything they want and we don't get a chance to refute it, and if we do, we look bad anyway. It's a no-win situation."

"We both know the truth, Christie. Now, let's work on these flowers for the college."

Lakeside Community College had developed an exchange program with a similar college in one of Tokyo's suburbs. Each year, ten or so Japanese students began a three-year nursing program. They were provided housing in an apartment building owned by the college, mentoring by bilingual advisors, and an excellent education.

The leadership team of their Tokyo-based college visited

Lakeside every three years to monitor and evaluate the program's success. Because the president of the college had been a high school mate of her father, she had been asked to provide the floral effects. She wanted her arrangements to be perfect and true to the original ikebana precepts.

She tucked the final bit of foliage into the shallow bowl and stood back to admire the finished product. "That, young lady, is beautiful," said Aunt Doris, who had stepped up behind her. "The Japanese visitors will be thoroughly impressed." She smiled and nodded at Christie's creation.

"I thought of making something more typical of our Pacific Northwest area, but I kept coming back to wanting to create a bouquet consistent with the culture of those young students."

Doris nodded and said, "The tabletop decorations for the other tables can be more typical of the region if you like. Or you can use local flowers in the Japanese style and cover both bases that way."

"That's a good idea, Auntie." Christie quickly sketched a drawing based on her aunt's suggestion. "We need ten of these for the reception this evening. Jason said he'd deliver them for me after work."

"Sounds good. I'll get the bowls ready with the florist foam while you select the blooms."

The two women worked quietly side by side for the next hour. Christie popped a CD of her favorite classical piano pieces into the Bose CD player. Aunt Doris hummed along.

The front door chimes tinkled merrily when they were almost done. Christie looked up to see a young woman enter the store, looking around as she took a couple of steps inside. She wore navy blue capris and a crisp white blouse and had sunglasses on her head and a leather tote on her shoulder. Her manner suggested someone of good taste.

"Welcome," called Christie. "I'll be right out." She wiped her hands on the towel on the counter and ran her hands through her curls. "How can I help you?"

The woman, whom Christie guessed to be in her twenties, smiled and said, "I was at Hailey's wedding last weekend. I loved her flowers and got your name from her mom. Hailey and Ryan are still on their honeymoon in the Bahamas, you know, so I couldn't ask her."

"Thank you," said Christie, smiling at the compliment.

"I'm getting married in September, and I was hoping to hire you to do the flowers for my wedding." Her smile was contagious. "Oh, I forgot my manners." She extended her hand. "I'm Leanne Cooper."

"Hi, Leanne. I'm Christie. Pleased to meet you." Christie nodded toward the middle of the room. "Let's go back to my desk and look at dates first, and then you can tell me what kind of budget you have and any ideas for flowers you might like. Does that sound okay?"

"Oh, yes! I don't want to copy Hailey, but after seeing what you did for her wedding, I'm sure you can do anything. I've been to a few weddings recently, and she definitely had the most beau tiful flowers."

Christie was starting to feel uncomfortable with all the superlatives but simply smiled and pulled out a wedding planner template for their discussion. After establishing the basics of date—which thankfully was not September fourteenth, Missy's wedding day, groom's name, budget, and ceremony and reception locations, the two of them looked through magazines and wedding books. Leanne shared some pictures on her phone from Hailey's reception that she particularly liked, as well as several from other sources.

Upon seeing a photo with the white hydrangeas, Christie said, "I recognize these from my tabletop arrangements at the country club. You have good taste, Leanne."

Her client beamed. Leanne zoomed in on the centerpiece in

one of the photos. "I love these huge, puffy flowers. My mom said they're hydrangeas."

Christie nodded. "Those are great blossoms to use in weddings. They're very dramatic and can be used in different ways, like the tabletop bouquets you see here."

"Is it okay if my mom and I come together in a day or two to talk to you? I know she has some ideas as well. And I can bring in some pictures from Pinterest as well, if that's okay."

"That's a great idea, Leanne. Seeing what you like will make it easier to create the look that you want for your own special day."

"Awesome. My mom said she worked here for your grandma when she was in high school."

"Is that right? What was her maiden name?"

"Annalisa Lassen. Did you know her?"

Aunt Doris called from the back of the shop. "Sure, I remember her. That was from before your time, Christie. She was always learning lines for a play or something or other, as I recall."

Leanne giggled. "She wanted to be a stage actress when she was young, but she said she discovered there was more money in bookkeeping."

"There's some truth in that," said Christie. "My degree is in accounting, but I'm having more fun here managing the shop that originally belonged to my grandma. Anyway, you and your mom can come by anytime. We're open till five on weekdays and till two on Saturdays."

Once Leanne was out the door, Christie let out a little squeal. "I love doing weddings!"

"I had a feeling you'd be getting more business once the public saw what you could do with that church and the country club," said her aunt. "Being young and having a good eye for design are advantages that you have when it comes to flowers for weddings."

"Well, I definitely won't be using any flower with the word 'belladonna' in it next time, whether or not it's beautiful." Christie penciled in the date for Leanne's wedding on her master planner. She didn't want to jinx herself by daring to use ink. She perused a couple of recent trade e-magazines on her computer, having remembered seeing some clever ideas for September weddings, and printed several pages. She'd already started a file folder labeled *Wedding Ideas* that she could refer to anytime.

She overheard her aunt in the flower room taking an order over the phone. It was an unconscious habit of hers to tune in when she heard the phone ring and to listen for a moment to see if she was needed. Most of the time, Aunt Doris took care of the order and that was that. Her ears perked up when she heard the name of a book and realized it was Deb from the bookstore.

"What was that all about, Auntie?" she asked when Doris ended the call.

"Deb at Books and More Books ordered a bouquet to go with that old book, *Champagne for One.* She's going to feature some of the books that your friendly reporter listed in that article. And she wants a fresh bouquet every week to go with each one. How about that?"

"Did she say what the poison was in that book? Was it belladonna?"

"No. She said it was cyanide in the champagne."

"Well, that's sweet of her, but it won't make up for losing other business if people are afraid of my flowers."

She turned back to her filing and was almost done when the front door chimed. Looking up and seeing Jason, she realized it was only a few minutes to closing time. She met him halfway across the room and hugged him briefly.

"Hi, Jason. You're right on time. We've just finished making the decorations for the college event."

He looked over her shoulder at the array of bowls and vases on the worktable in the flower room. "Those are fabulous!"

Christie grinned. That was a major statement coming from a guy, although she'd noticed over the last several months that he had a good eye for design and balance. And willingly shared compliments.

"The three of us can load them into the shop's van, and then I'll meet you at the event center. There will be some students there who can help us unload and transfer these indoors. Okay?"

"Only if I get to take you out for Wednesday night tacos at the Silver Spoon Saloon afterward. Nathan and Anita are going to meet us there."

"What if I have other plans already?" Christie teased, but secretly glad he'd felt comfortable inviting her for an impromptu night out.

"Well, I kinda checked with your aunt first to make sure you didn't have a meeting or something important on your calendar," Jason replied softly, his face reddening.

Christie turned to her aunt. "And you kept it a secret! I'm impressed."

"You're not mad, are you, Christie?" said her aunt. "It seemed harmless and very sweet of him to want to surprise you."

"Of course not. I'm flattered. Now, let's get these decorations in the van before I change my mind about tacos."

Christie did feel flattered, in a way, but a niggling part of her also huffed at being taken for granted, even if it was from two of the important people in her life. But it wasn't like a date, exactly. Not with Anita and Nathan there as well, right?

CHAPTER 16

fter delivering the flowers to the college, Christie and Jason met Anita and Nathan at the Silver Spoon Saloon. The popular pub had recently started featuring inexpensive tacos on Wednesday nights, following a trend in the local community. Tuesdays and Wednesdays were typically slow nights at bars and pubs and even restaurants in general. Cheap tacos or "buffalo wings, " depending on the day, were the enticement to get people in the doors, with money being made on higher-profit beer and wine and mixed drinks. The foursome sat at a cozy high-top table in a corner of the room.

"This feels like another meeting of Sherlock Holmes wannabes," said Anita.

"Or maybe a cheap date night," said Jason.

Christie felt herself squirm at the 'date' reference but tried not to show it.

"I want to know the latest news on your killer flowers, Christie," said Nathan.

"And I want my flowers not referred to as 'killer.' As well as two crispy chicken tacos with a pint of Manny's pale ale," said Christie, at which everyone laughed.

After ordering a round of tacos, pub chips, and a pitcher of beer, Christie briefed everyone on the latest information from Conway.

"He didn't indicate who else he had in mind as the suspect," said Christie, "assuming Cameron was the real target. Well, he kind of suggested that Nathan might have been angry enough to do the deed." She grimaced as Nathan sat back, shocked at the suggestion. "I had to remind him that Nathan would have had to have the poison in his pocket. And he would have been angry at his cousin Aaron, not Cameron. Conway hasn't mentioned if he thought there might have been any other targets."

"Yeah, especially since he doesn't know what the actual substance was," said Jason.

Anita nudged Nathan. "Tell them what you told me about Aaron."

Nathan did an eye roll and swallowed before speaking. "Aaron has still been saying he doesn't have any more information to give the doctors at the hospital. Uncle Conan thinks he knows something and won't admit it."

"Hmm. Perhaps it's something that incriminates himself," said Christie.

"Or someone else," offered Jason. "Why does your uncle think Aaron's hiding something? Other than saying he doesn't know anything, I mean."

"For one thing, Aaron was late getting to the church for the pictures before the wedding. Hailey was practically in tears over it, and Ryan, the groom, was ready to start the photo session even though they were missing a groomsman."

"That doesn't sound like much," said Jason.

"Not by itself, but when Uncle Conan said something about his being irresponsible, Aunt Michelle made some comment about his having to run an errand."

"Michelle was defending him?" asked Christie. "Didn't

someone say she was unhappy that Aaron was invited to be a groomsman in the first place?"

"Exactly," said Nathan. "Of course, at the time, no one asked her what errand that might be."

Jason had a quizzical look on his face. "Why were *you* there for the pictures, Nathan? You weren't a groomsman, were you?"

"No, but with so many of the family being together for the wedding anyway, Aunt Michelle wanted to have family photos in addition to the wedding pictures. So we all obliged."

"That makes sense," said Christie. "I'd probably do the same thing. But it's hard to make Aaron's being late into something sinister."

"I'm with you on that, Christie," said Jason. "His unwillingness to offer more help is more worrisome to me, speaking from an attorney's perspective, of course."

Christie used the break in the conversation to share the news about the society news story in the Herald Falls paper. "The only good part is that the bookstore ordered a bouquet of flowers to go along with one of the books. And a fresh bouquet each week while she runs this promotion."

Anita reached across the table and patted Christie on the arm. "Maybe there will be a silver lining in this. Other young women will see the name of your shop in the article, and you may get more wedding business. Plus, your flowers will be displayed at the bookstore."

"I was more worried that potential customers would shy away from my flowers," said Christie.

"People who care about society, like the Michelle Starrs of the world, like to copy others. So, if your flowers were good enough for her, they're more likely to follow suit."

"I hadn't thought of it that way," admitted Christie. "Madison, the young reporter, did say the flowers were beautiful."

"See?" Anita clapped her hands. "There you go."

The talk petered out when the waitress brought their order. A tray of condiments—sour cream, hot salsa, green chili sauce and olives—accompanied the baskets of hot tacos in addition to a bowl of *queso* for dipping the pub chips. They ate hungrily until there was only a handful of chips on the platter. Jason and Nathan were matching each other, eating chip for chip until there was only one left. Christie quickly grabbed it and ate it, grinning broadly, thus avoiding a friendly argument over who was going to get to eat it.

Jason said, "Going back to the Starr family, Nathan, how do you and your uncle Conan manage to stay civil with each other over those complaints you are investigating at the nuclear plant? Isn't it hard to have to be objective with someone you're related to?"

Nathan set his glass down. "I'm not evaluating my uncle per se. My job is to investigate the claims that were submitted to the NRC. First, I have to determine if the complaint is even valid, which is why I request multiple reports so I can see if there is anything to substantiate the concern. Once I make a decision that there either is or is not a potential legitimate incident, I request more information and follow all the bunny trails and timelines from the alleged incident forward and backward."

"It sounds tedious," said Christie.

"It is," said Nathan. "But it's the only way to determine whether or not the NRC needs to step in."

"I'm assuming your uncle understands this," said Jason, "and that's why he seems less anxious about it than your aunt."

"Exactly. Aunt Michelle apparently believes my job is to discredit her husband instead of evaluating the validity of any complaints."

"Maybe she wishes it were *you* who collapsed instead of Cameron," said Christie.

"Christie!" said Anita, "It's not nice to even *think* that."

"You know I didn't mean that I thought Nathan *should* collapse," said Christie. "I was just wondering if Michelle was thinking that would have been *her* preference. Maybe the poison was meant for Nathan, and somehow Cameron got it instead."

Nathan held up his hand in "halt" mode. "Aunt Michelle has been under a lot of stress with the wedding. She's been trying to accommodate the groom's mom's preferences, which had been made explicitly clear a while back. And then the complaints at the nuclear plant have added to her list of concerns." He shook his head. "She really is a nice person, most of the time."

"Christie's cat hissed at her at the shop," said Anita.

The two men looked at each other, uncertain of what Anita was getting at.

"Which probably doesn't mean anything, Anita," said Christie. "Stormy's a cat and probably doesn't have ESP."

"Then how do service dogs sense when their owners are about to have a seizure or get severely low blood sugar?" Anita argued.

"They're trained to do that," said Christie with a giggle, "and they're dogs smelling medical conditions, not cats having, well, hissy fits."

Nathan jumped in. "My grandma taught her cat to jump through her arms when she held them out like a hoop. She would say, 'Jump, Hansel,' and Hansel would jump through her arms. It was quite entertaining."

Christie giggled. "That's clever, but it's still not ESP. Anyway, speaking of the shop reminds me of a young lady who came in today. She asked me to do the flowers for her wedding in September. She was at Hailey's ceremony and loved what she saw. She even took photos to show me some of the flowers she especially liked, like the white hydrangeas."

"Those were my favorites, too," said Anita. "By the way, did you remember to take photos of the candelabra and the arch for your wedding file?"

Christie straightened her shoulders and said smugly, "Yes, I did. Although I admit that Aunt Doris also reminded me, or I might not have thought of it. In fact, I just realized that one of the photos that Leanne, the bride-to-be, showed me had Nathan in it. I only saw the back side of his right arm and shoulder, but I knew it was him because I recognized the dress Anita was wearing as she sat on the other side of him."

"Oh," said Anita. "I remember someone coming up and asking us to scoot to the side so she could take a better picture of the decorations. That must have been your new client."

Christie nodded as she swallowed her beer. "I might ask her to forward a few of her photos to me so I can add them to my website. She's coming in later this week with her mom to talk budgets, venues, and so forth."

"Aren't digital cameras wonderful for that kind of sharing?" said Anita. "Although they have put companies like Kodak and Polaroid on life support, if they even still exist."

"Survival of the fittest," said Jason. He turned to Christie, and asked, "Aren't you going to tell them about Missy and Brian?"

"Missy? What about Missy?" asked Anita, eyes wide.

"Well, Missy called today and said she and Brian are getting married in September. That'll be two weddings in one month!"

"And I'm sure there will be more to follow," said Anita.

"Unless I lose my business over this Cameron affair."

CHAPTER 17

id-morning the next day, Christie looked up from her desk when the door chime sounded. She watched as two women entered. She smiled broadly when she recognized Leanne and got up from her chair to meet them.

"Hi, Leanne. This must be your mother," she said, offering her hand to the other woman. "I'm Christie O'Mara. I'm so pleased to meet you."

"Yes, I'm Annalisa Cooper. Leanne was so excited when she saw your flowers at Hailey's wedding and couldn't wait to get me down here. She said she told you I worked for your grandmother when I was in school. I'm glad you decided to re-open the business."

Christie smiled, saying, "So am I. Come with me."

Christie led the way to the back of the shop, where she had created a consultation area to meet with clients. Several bridal magazines, a notebook of floral ideas and a vase with fresh flowers sat on top of a charming wooden desk from her own teenage bedroom. She smiled at the memory of sitting at the desk and daydreaming of the future, never thinking this desk would grace her very own flower shop.

"This is lovely," said Mrs. Cooper, looking around the shop. "Not surprising, of course. Leanne showed me pictures from the church and country club. Your decorations were fabulous."

Christie felt her face warm. "Thank you. It was fun to create a tropical island experience here in the Pacific Northwest. As well as challenging."

"Well, we don't want anything so fancy as that, I don't think. Isn't that right, Leanne?" she asked, turning to her daughter.

Leanne pulled up the photos from her phone again and zoomed in on the white hydrangeas. "This is what I love. I want to feel like we're in the clouds, and everything is white and beautiful."

"That's a lovely idea, Leanne," said Christie. "It won't be nearly as expensive as those tropical flowers, either." Christie fished out a business card from one of the drawers. "I'd love to have some of those photos myself if you don't mind sending them when you get a minute. I want to have a portfolio to show prospective clients like you." She quickly wrote down her cell number on the back of the card.

"I'd be happy to," said Leanne, her face beaming.

"We're prepared to pay a fair price for the flowers, of course," said the mom. "I've done some research, and I know what weddings cost these days." She widened her eyes.

"Well, Mrs. Cooper. I'm sure I can—"

"Oh, please call me Annalisa. Mrs. Cooper makes me feel old."

"Of course, Annalisa. I can work with the budget that Leanne gave me earlier and create a magical wedding for your daughter."

"That's what Leanne and I were hoping to hear," said Annalisa. "I have to admit, we've visited a couple of other florists and were surprised at what they wanted to charge. Appalled, even."

"Like I said, I know what it's like to manage on a budget,"

said Christie. "Why don't you two look through these folders and put post-it tabs on the pictures that you like? I'll give you fifteen or twenty minutes while I take care of some business."

"Perfect," the mom and daughter said simultaneously.

Christie popped in a CD of music appropriate for a wedding reception and smiled to herself at her cleverness. The music was supposed to create a mood for the bride-to-be as she planned her wedding arrangements, whether it was the flowers or some other aspect. She'd picked up the idea from one of the blogs she'd run across.

"Christie, can you help me back here, please?" called Aunt Doris.

Her aunt was working on a huge bouquet ordered for a chamber of commerce "meet and greet" event by one of the banks that were hosting the evening. The chrysanthemums and *alstroemeria* were in shades of peach and crimson, which coordinated nicely with creamy white roses against a background of blue-green eucalyptus and other greenery.

"That's absolutely gorgeous!" Christie exclaimed. "What kind of help do you need?"

"I can't decide which of these ribbons would be best." Ribbons of different colors and widths lay on the counter next to the vase.

Christie studied the options for a moment, then selected a three-inch wide ecru ribbon edged with burgundy. "This one is elegant and pulls in a couple of the other colors. Would you like me to make the bow for you?"

"Certainly. I'll add a few more roses, and this one will be ready for Heather to deliver as soon as she gets here after school."

A few minutes later, Christie turned her head and noticed that Leanne and Annalisa were looking her way. She joined them at the table. "Did you find something you like?"

Leanne leafed through the pages she'd marked. "Can you do something that looks like these pictures?"

The inspiration photos she'd marked had a classic, ethereal look. Christie nodded happily. "Absolutely. I'll work up some sketches and a preliminary cost estimate within Leanne's budget and get back to you in a week or two. Will that work?"

After the two ladies had departed, Christie scrolled through her messages to see if the photos had landed. She'd heard a few pings while she was working with the ribbon for the bank bouquet. She wanted to print up the best ones for her wedding planner portfolio before she forgot all about it. The majority of them had been taken at Hailey's reception at the country club, and were of the tabletop bouquets taken from different angles, as expected. Leanne had apparently wanted to capture as much detail as possible. There were a few photos of the buffet table and of the wedding cake, as well as several images of the arch at the church. Christie selected a few of them to print on her store printer for future reference. She planned to have them printed on proper photo paper as well at one of the local print shops for a more professional finish.

She started sliding the prints into clear sleeves for her folder. When she got to the third print, she noticed that the punch cup on one of the tables had something dark in it. She compared the images and realized it was the only glass that appeared to contain blueberries. She wondered if had anything to do with the tropical theme, although she didn't think blueberries grew in that climate. Perhaps there was some other significance to the berries.

"I wonder if Anita would remember what kind of drinks were being served," she asked herself aloud. "And if she noticed blueberries in any of them."

Stormy opened an eye in response to her voice and stretched. Christie reached up and scratched her behind the ears. "Only one way to find out." She sent a quick text to Anita, who was still at school, and studied the photos again. She identified several glasses on other tables in the photos, some with the traditional pineapple spears and maraschino cherries, but none of the other glasses had blueberries in them.

CHAPTER 18

$\mathcal{A}$nita called during her lunch break. "Why do you want to know what kind of drinks were at the reception?"

Christie described what she'd seen in the photographs.

"Okay. Here's what I remember," said Anita. "When we first got there, we were offered a tropical drink that reminded me of a cosmopolitan. Or we were told we could get something at the bar. Nathan went for scotch, I think, and I had a glass of pinot grigio. There was also a champagne toast, but that was toward the middle of the affair."

"Did any of the tropical drinks have any berries in them?"

"I don't know about drinks at the bar itself," said Anita, "but there were punch bowls set up across the room. I noticed that one was spiked and one wasn't and that the glasses in front of the spiked bowl had blueberries in them. I assume that was a way to tell which ones were alcoholic."

"That would make sense," replied Christie. "I suppose a call to the catering department at the country club would be the next step."

"Good idea. Gotta run. Five minutes till afternoon chaos begins."

. . .

CHRISTIE LOOKED up the number for the club. Unfortunately, the caterer was out until Friday. She wrote herself a note to call the next day.

After lunch, the phone was busy with calls for corsages and boutonnieres for the final dance of the school year. Christie had obtained a school calendar courtesy of Anita several months prior, after having been caught unprepared for a dance in March and having to scramble to have enough flowers for the last-minute orders for boutonniere and corsages.

During her first six months of business, she had noticed a rhythm of sorts with peaks of orders around Christmas, Valentine's Day, Easter and Mother's Day, followed by troughs that were punctuated by birthdays, anniversaries, and, of course, funerals. She anticipated a slowing of orders for bouquets during the summer but hoped sales of her gift items and the small pieces of vintage furniture would be enough to get her through the rest of her first full year of business.

Earlier, she had found her grandmother's records of sales and receipts in the storage room, which confirmed her observation of the pattern. Unless something drastic happened—like being accused of murder, heaven forbid—she expected to stay profitable until November rolled around again and she began a new cycle.

The door chimed, announcing a visitor. Christie looked up to see Chief Conway saunter in, headed her way.

"Good afternoon, Christie," he said. "Got a minute?"

Christie set aside her animosity toward the chief and pasted a smile on her face as she rose to greet him. "Of course, Chief. Do you have some good news?"

"I'm not sure I'd call it that." He frowned and reached into his shirt pocket. "I just got a call from the hospital about the young man who collapsed at that wedding. He seems to be getting better, but his friend Aaron is not."

"What's wrong with Aaron? He didn't appear to be sick earlier."

"He's making comments to the nursing staff about how Cameron should be off the ventilator by now, and when are they going to start him on strengthening therapy, and stuff like that."

"What does that have to do with me?" asked Christie, confused. "That sounds like a risk management issue, perhaps."

"Yeah, I said the same thing." Conway turned his hat in his hand. "One of the team who has been his primary nurse the past three days said Aaron's behavior seems to be what she calls 'decompensating.' If you don't know, it means the failure to cope well in response to stress, which can be indicative of other ongoing issues. Basically, she said he's been more agitated. And, as you know, he hasn't been answering our questions fully, or those from the doctors in the intensive care unit."

"So, the nurse is just going on a gut feeling, do you think?" Christie asked.

"Yeah, but I have a feeling she's right. I just can't prove it yet."

Christie frowned. "So, again, what does that have to do with me? I certainly don't have any medical expertise."

"Right. But there's another thing that you might be able to help with. He asked the nurse about the jacket that Cameron was wearing the night of the reception. He wanted to get it back. She told him all his belongings were put into a plastic bag in the emergency room and normally would have gone with him to the ICU. But they don't have anything of his there now. So, as far as she knew, the belongings would have been given to the family in the ER. Of course, he got mad about that."

"Did he go to the emergency room and track it down that way?" Christie asked.

"He did, but the staff there didn't have it anymore. They also told him anything in his possession went with Cameron to the ICU."

"He probably feels like he's getting the runaround," said Christie. "Could someone else from the family have taken charge of the bag? Like Michelle or Conan Starr?"

"I'm going to check with them after I leave here," said Conway. "But I wondered, since it wasn't in the ICU or the ER, maybe it never made it to the hospital at all. I came here first in case the jacket ended up in your flower bins or boxes when you cleaned up from the reception."

Christie cocked her head. "No. He was still wearing one when he collapsed at the country club. I remember because he was wearing a boutonniere like the groomsmen. Maybe it ended up in the ambulance. The EMTs would have had to get access to his arm to start an IV, and, in the movies, at least, I've seen them cut clothes off to do that." She shrugged.

"Great idea!" Conway slapped the desk with his hand. "I hadn't thought of that. I'll check with the hospital and find out which ambulance company took him in."

Stormy jumped down at the sudden noise and put her head up to Conway's hand for a scratch behind the ears. Christie picked up her kitty and kissed her on the nose as she waited for Conway to exit, happy he was gone on a mission.

Then she asked Stormy, "That's the second time I've heard about that jacket. Now, why would Aaron care about a jacket? Especially since it's basically unwearable after being cut off Cameron's body."

CHAPTER 19

$\mathcal{A}$nita called while Christie was putting dishes away after eating a dinner of warmed-over King's ranch casserole, courtesy of her mom.

"Do you mind if Nathan and I come over? He wants to ask you something about Cameron."

"Can't he ask me over the phone?"

"He said he'd rather do it in person but didn't explain why."

"Sure. Come on over."

Christie filled a plate with her mom's homemade cookies that had accompanied the casserole and grabbed a bottle of Italian Sangiovese that Jason had given her a few days earlier. Stormy joined her at the door a few minutes later when the doorbell sang its tune of "When Irish Eyes are Smiling." Christie swooped up her kitty before opening the door. "No mouse hunting tonight, Stormy. We have company."

Nathan held a bottle of cabernet sauvignon in his hand and Anita carried a box of chocolates from the chocolatier who had a shop two doors down from Christie's Flower Shoppe.

Christie laughed. "Those look like bribes. I can hardly wait to hear what you have to say, Nathan."

A bit later, settled and sated with the cabernet wine and excellent cookies, Nathan began. "As you know, I've been looking into the threats—or complaints, if you will—that Uncle Conan has received at the nuclear plant."

Christie pulled her legs under her on the chair where she was sitting. "Are you sure you can talk to me about those? Isn't that secret?"

"Actually, no. I can't tell you *what* I learn during the investigation, but reporting the fact that the threats have been made is not privileged information. In fact, I need to ask you some questions that relate directly to the threats because you had a few minutes with Aaron and Cameron at the reception."

"What does that have to do with the nuclear plant?"

Christie caught a brief look that passed between Anita and Nathan.

"This isn't public information, but it's not exactly secret either, so I'm going to share it with you," said Nathan. "There's one particular organization that targets nuclear plants regularly with threats and various complaints. The NRC is familiar with their style, and our agents are usually able to identify those complaints as false fairly quickly."

"Are you saying that this anti-nuclear group is responsible for filing the local complaints?"

"Not exactly, although I haven't been able to fully dismiss the latest one as coming from one of their sites. There are some subtle differences with the most recent complaint, and I'm beginning to think there's a copycat group targeting the Omega Nuclear facility."

"Okay, but what does that have to do with Aaron or Cameron or me?" Christie stroked Stormy's silken fur as she listened.

"At the end of the reception, you said that Aaron came in looking for Cameron. Correct?"

"Yes. We were just starting to clear out the flowers from the tables when he burst through the door."

"When did you find Cameron?"

Christie cocked her head. "It was less than a minute later, I think, that Heather yelled for 911. She found him lying on the floor by one of the tables."

"This is important, Christie, so try to recall anything that Aaron said when he got there."

Christie closed her eyes, recalling the moment. "He didn't say much. He called out Cameron's name, and he asked me if I'd seen him. Of course, I didn't know who it was yet. When Heather found him, he said Cameron was his best friend, but I swear he started to say the word 'partner' before he corrected himself. And he told me his name when I asked, and that's about it."

"Are you sure he didn't say anything else?"

"Um. Nothing particular.'" Christie shook her head. "That's all I can remember."

"Did you overhear any conversation he had with the EMTs?"

Christie closed her eyes again for a moment. "He gave them Cameron's age, birth date, and that kind of thing. They asked about any health issues and allergies and he denied any problems." She frowned. "What kind of information are you looking for? I don't understand how what I might have heard might be useful."

"Did you possibly hear where Aaron and Cameron live? I know they don't live near here, and even though Aaron is my cousin, we've never been close. His dad and my dad had a falling out years ago about Aaron being gay. My dad said some pretty nasty things about Aaron being gay at the time. And Dad's attitude on gays hasn't changed in the meantime." Nathan shrugged. "Plus, Doyle isn't the forgiving type. Aaron basically doesn't acknowledge me, although I don't personally have a problem with Aaron and Cameron being partners."

"Why does it matter where they live? Can't you ask Aaron? Or someone else in the family?"

Nathan replied, "Hailey knows, but she's on her honeymoon, and I'm not going to try to ask her."

"I bet your aunt knows. She seemed pretty tight with her daughter. And of course she would have a copy of the mailing list for the wedding invitations."

Nathan nodded. "She would normally be the logical person to ask. In this case, I haven't wanted to ask Uncle Conan because he's right in the middle of the whole thing, and I'm not exactly on Aunt Michelle's list of favorite people right now because of what I do and the recent threats. But I would hope she would answer my question as part of the probe into the threats."

"Why do you need to know where they live in the first place?" asked Christie. "How is that helpful?"

"That's the part I can't tell you yet because I don't actually know." Nathan shrugged as if in apology. They all fell silent for a few minutes as they finished their refreshments. "Good cookies, by the way," Nathan finally said, and Christie knew she wouldn't get more out of him about the case.

After Anita and Nathan left, Christie sat with Stormy on her lap in front of the fireplace. It was unlit because it had been a warm day. The cat purred while Christie mulled over the conversation with Nathan. Something he had said about public versus investigative information puzzled her. She called Jason in case he could shed some light on her curiosity.

"How's the amateur detective holding up?" Jason asked when she called.

"I'm okay. That's kind of why I'm calling. Nathan and Anita just left." She briefed Jason on the conversation. "Now I'm curious about the difference between what information would be considered okay to share with the public in a situation like this and what's considered investigative."

"That's an interesting question, and I don't know the answer. I'll have to do a bit of investigating myself on what you shared before I can tell you."

"I was surprised that Nathan doesn't know where Aaron, his own cousin, lives," said Christie. "It seems like someone who works for a government agency would have all kinds of resources at hand instead of asking someone like me if I've overheard the information. Then, when I specifically asked, he said he couldn't tell me why it might be helpful to him."

"Which means it *is* important to his current investigation," said Jason. "Now I'm curious, too. I'll see what I can find out."

CHAPTER 20

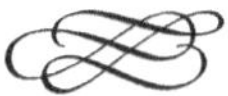

Christie felt a chill Friday morning when she opened the back door of her shop. As she hung up her jacket, she saw Aunt Doris sitting at her worktable with her head in her hands.

Christie rushed over to her aunt after lifting Stormy up to her perch. "What's wrong, Auntie? Are you not feeling well?"

Aunt Doris lifted her arm and pointed to the front of the store. "Look at the window."

Christie walked slowly toward the entrance and saw that something had been spray-painted in red on the outside of the window. It took her a moment to read it in reverse. She read aloud, "Murderer." She held her hands to her face, anger prickling her, and shouted, "I'm calling Chief Conway."

"No need. He's on his way," said her aunt quietly. "I called him as soon as I saw it."

Then her anger drained to dread. "Do you suppose Cameron died?"

Her aunt shook her head. "I haven't heard, but maybe so."

Every fiber of Christie tingled, and she needed to do something, now, so she picked up her phone and went out the entrance door. "I'll take a picture of it in case I need it for insurance."

Chief Conway pulled up in front of the shop while she snapped a few photos, her anger and dread turning to exasperation.

"Good idea, Christie," he said when he was out of the cruiser. "I was planning to do the same thing. I'll have one of the officers come over and wash that off for you. We've had some practice in cleaning up graffiti over the years."

Christie managed a bleak smile before starting to ask a question, but a sob prevented more than a gasp.

Conway handed her a wadded-up handkerchief as he said, "No, Cameron's still alive, if that's what you're wondering. Let's go inside. McAvoy is on his way with the clean-up kit."

"Here's some tea to warm you up," said Aunt Doris once they sat down at the worktable.

"Thank you," said Conway. "I suspect the culprit is Aaron, or maybe he had someone do his dirty work, but he's just lashing out at you, Christie."

"Are you sure Cameron's still alive?"

"I called the hospital as soon as your aunt notified me. In fact, he's getting better and might get off the ventilator in the next twenty-four hours."

Christie breathed a sigh of relief. "So, if it's Aaron, why would he call me a murderer?"

Conway shrugged. "I wish I knew the answer to that. But I told you he's probably acting out and isn't coping well."

"Okay." Christie inhaled deeply, trying to stay calm. "Another question on a different topic. Did you find the jacket yet?"

"Now, there's some good news. Yesterday, you suggested checking with the ambulance companies. Fortunately, there are only three companies around here to call. Turns out that it was in the ambulance after all. It had stayed on the EMT's gurney when

Cameron was transferred to the emergency room gurney and nobody noticed it until they cleaned up their gear later. They weren't sure what to do with it until McAvoy called them. Anyway, he picked it up late yesterday and delivered it to the evidence lab after he showed it to me."

"Are you sure it was the right one?"

"Yep. I recognized the purple flower in the lapel, although it was really wilted and in bad shape. I think you called it a calla lily."

Christie smiled at the chief's recall of the boutonniere flower's name. "Very good, Chief. I'm impressed that you remembered. Do you want a job here?"

"Nah. I'm good." He looked up and saw a second cruiser parked in front of the shop. "Looks like McAvoy's here. I'll go help him clean up the window."

"Thanks. I'll keep my fingers crossed for Cameron."

Christie's shoulders sagged when she walked back to the flower room. Aunt Doris was still sitting at the worktable with a worried look on her face.

"What is it, Auntie? Conway and McAvoy are cleaning up the window already."

Her aunt held up the newest issue of the local weekly newspaper. "You made the front page of the paper."

Killer Flowers Strike Again. Christie gasped and covered her mouth. "No! Not now!" She dropped onto the stool on the other side of the table, one hand holding the newspaper, the other over her mouth as she read the lead article.

"This isn't even true," she finally said. "My flowers didn't kill anyone last fall, and this time, no one died yet."

"But your business might die," said Aunt Doris, "regardless of the truth."

. . .

JASON CAME by the shop midday. Christie had sent her aunt home for lunch during the typically slow hour between one and two p.m.

"Hey. What brings you in here today?" Christie asked, looking up from her desk behind the sales counter. "Are you going to tell me about this morning's paper?"

"No, but my receptionist brought it into the office and made sure I read it. She knows I don't usually look at it till I get home after work." Jason leaned on an elbow in front of her. "It's just gossip for now," he added.

"It's still not good for business. Conway needs to figure out the rest of the story so they can publish a retraction. Soon." Christie slammed her fist on the counter. When Jason cringed, she said, "I'm sorry, Jason. I'm frustrated with the newspaper, not you." She inhaled a lungful of air. "Now, if it's not about the paper, why *are* you here?"

"Well, I wanted to share what I found out this morning when I looked into complaints to the Nuclear Regulatory Commission."

Christie jumped up from her chair. "Do tell!"

"You've probably seen in the news that there are all kinds of do-gooders and terrorist groups and other sorts who post comments and complaints about almost anything they disagree with. Nuclear plants are one of those targets, as you know."

"Yeah. No surprise there."

"The Omega plant in our own backyard, so to speak, has been targeted regularly by several different groups that complain and make noise, but they never rise to the point of being serious enough to cause concern."

Christie nodded. "Nathan mentioned something like that when he was telling us about his work here. I'm guessing you're going to tell me that something has changed."

"Correct. From all indications, there seems to be a new group or organization that has not only been filing complaints but making threats that are more plausible than in the past. And that makes them more worrisome if I'm reading between the lines accurately."

"And?"

"While I can't go deeper to find any information beyond what is available to the public, my gut feeling is that there's an inside person at the plant involved in the recent development. Or maybe it seems that way because of how the latest letter was worded."

Christie raised an eyebrow. "If *you* get that sense, then Conan Starr, the manager, must feel the same way. And Nathan, too."

"Maybe even Michelle, if Conan has shared anything at all with his wife."

"He wouldn't share specifics, I would think," said Christie, "but Michelle probably knows him well enough to be able to tell when something is wrong without him telling her exactly what is."

"I agree," said Jason. "And that's probably why Nathan has been requesting so much information. He's most likely looking for a pattern that will lead him to the guilty party. False complaints are one thing, but this group appears to be as much into threats as well."

"That's scary to think about," Christie said, shuddering. "Even scarier than waiting for our friendly volcano to erupt again. You do realize, don't you, that the Omega facility is only fifteen miles away via that proverbial crow, whereas Mt. St. Helens is about thirty miles away. That's twice as far."

"Yes, and a nuclear disaster is likely to cause a wider circle of damage."

"True." Christie leaned both elbows on the counter, chin in hands. "No wonder Nathan is working hard to find the source of the threats. Do you suppose he's interviewed his uncle?"

"Oh, yeah. I'm sure Conan Starr was the first person on his

list. And everyone who reports directly to him and on down the management chain."

"I sure hope he figures out who's at the bottom of this before long," said Christie. "If the nuclear plant blows up, I won't have to worry about a lawsuit from Aaron about Cameron. I won't have a business anyway. White Castle will be a ghost town." Christie picked up the paper, glanced at the headline again, then pushed the paper toward Jason with a grimace. She managed a smile as she said, "As long as you're here, I'll ask if we are still on for tonight."

"Considering the town hasn't blown up yet, yes," he replied. "Nathan and Anita are planning to meet us at the Rock at six. We're skipping a movie after all, if that's okay. And I hope you don't mind driving yourself. I'm never sure of timing when I have to make a court appearance."

CHAPTER 21

ith the shop quiet for a few moments and with Doris back from lunch to handle the phone, Christie pulled out her wedding folio and studied the pictures from Hailey's reception again. Noticing the berries in that glass again reminded her that she had planned to call the caterer at the country club about the drinks and that Enrico should be there now, according to the young woman who had answered the phone Thursday.

Enrico's thick Italian accent boomed through the phone when he answered. "How may I help you? Lauren says you asked about a menu item."

"Yes, that's correct. Last Saturday your wait staff served a drink at the Starr-Edwards reception that may have been some kind of punch."

"Punch?" He scoffed. "Italian chefs don't make punch. That's for church meetings and children's parties. Not for weddings."

"Yes, sir. I'm not sure what it was, but it was red in color and was served at the country club for Hailey Starr's reception. Do you remember what it would have been? Please?"

Enrico chortled. "Will you believe this? Hailey's mother wanted to have cranberry and vodka with fresh berries for the drink. I tell her she must use something that is sparkling with the juice, a white wine like prosecco or Asti Spumante if she wanted to add fresh berries so they complement better, but she insisted that her friends would like the vodka better."

Christie suppressed a giggle at Enrico's disdain and his insistence that the Italian white wines would pair better with juice and berries. A momentary thought crossed her mind that too many glassfuls of cranberry and vodka might have caused more than one church lady to collapse. And wondered if it contributed to Cameron's collapse. She frowned. But Conway said Michelle insisted she'd made it clear that the glass she'd seen without berries was non-alcoholic because Cameron didn't drink.

"Hey, Enrico. I agree with you about using wine. But you said cranberries? I saw one glass in a picture that had a few blueberries in the bottom of the glass."

She heard him huff. "If I use berries with cranberry juice, it must be cranberries. Maybe it wasn't the punch, as you call it. There was an open bar, and people could order whatever was on the drinks menu."

"That's a thought," said Christie. "I can check with the head bartender and ask what options were offered to the guests. Thank you, Enrico. I hope to meet you in person someday in the future. You sound like a fun person."

"Humph. You are welcome. You come to the club, and I will fix you a proper drink. Ciao."

Christie giggled into the phone as the call ended. She could picture Michelle and Enrico going back and forth on menu items, with Michelle winning most of the arguments. She was footing the bill, after all, or at least, hubby Conan Starr was. Her next call was to the bartender at the club. Mike assured her that nobody had any berries added to their drink during the reception in question. But there was a possibility that berries were added to the caterer's punch without his knowledge. Having already asked Enrico about what he served, Christie found herself at a dead end in her quest. Perhaps they didn't mean anything after all, although she liked Anita's suggestion that they were meant to differentiate the two bowls of punch.

What started as a quiet Friday afternoon turned semi-chaotic when the teenage boys and girls came in twos and threes, picking up their corsages and boutonnieres for the last Friday night dance of the school year.

Christie was engrossed in entering the day's receipts into her accounting menu after the final corsage purchase when the front door chimed. She looked up to see Aaron enter. His face was red with a scowl and his arms looked stiff, like he was ready for a fight. He looked around for a few seconds before approaching the sales counter in the center of the shop.

Christie pulled herself up to her full five feet four inches as he neared her workspace. "How can I help you, Mr. Starr?" Out of the corner of her eye, she noticed Doris move furtively from her worktable in the flower room to the storage room at the back of the shop. Stormy jumped down from her shelf and sat squarely in front of Christie facing Aaron, her hackles up and tail slowly twitching back and forth.

When Aaron was a couple of feet away from the desk, Stormy stood and arched her back. She hissed, and her black fur bristled as she began walking back and forth in front of her owner, tail flicking angrily. Christie reached out and scratched behind her kitty's ears. Stormy stopped pacing but maintained her protective posture.

Aaron jumped back a few inches. "Is your cat dangerous?"

"I don't think so. She's just reacting to your mood." Christie picked up her cat and held her closely. "How can I help you, Aaron?"

"I want to warn you that my attorney is getting ready to put your flower shop out of business if Cameron doesn't come out of this."

Christie swallowed the lump in her throat. "Chief Conway said that Cameron is getting better and might be off the ventilator soon. That sounds like a good sign."

Aaron waved a hand in the air. "That's not the same thing as being fully recovered. The doctors in this hillbilly place said they don't know if he'll have brain damage or be able to walk or... or..." He began sobbing and wiped tears away with his jacket sleeve.

Christie reached out from behind the desk and offered him a box of tissues.

He grabbed the box and yanked several tissues out.

"I'm so sorry about your friend," said Christie, "but it's probably too early to tell if he's going to get all the way well or not." She caught a glimpse of a cruiser pulling into a parking spot in front of her shop. "Doctors aren't fortune tellers, and they can't promise anything at this stage."

Doris had emerged from the back and brought one of the chairs from Christie's consultation corner for Aaron. She invited him to sit down.

He glanced at the smiling, frizzy-headed woman and sat down. "Thanks." He sniffled, his whole demeanor collapsing in on himself. "Yeah. I know you're right, but I can't imagine life without Cameron. I don't want to even try." Aaron turned his head toward the door when he heard the chime. "I'd better go." He stood and started to walk away from the counter.

Conway entered and quickly assessed the situation. "Hey, Christie. How's business today?"

"Just like any Friday, Chief," she replied. "Are you making your afternoon rounds?"

"You bet," Conway said as he approached Christie and Aaron, who still stood next to the chair. "Just making sure the bad guys don't try anything stupid around here." He looked directly at Aaron, who stared at the floor. "I just got a call from the hospital. Your friend is breathing on his own. You might want to go visit him. Maybe take him some flowers from our favorite florist." He looked cautiously at Christie.

"On it," Doris called from her worktable.

"Uh, yes, sir," said Aaron, looking up to meet Conway's eyes. "That's a good idea." He began fumbling for a wallet.

Christie waved off his offer to pay. "These are on me. I'm pretty sure fresh flowers aren't allowed in the ICU, but I'll bet the nurses would be glad to enjoy them until Cameron goes to a regular ward. They'll even transfer the flowers to his new room for him."

"Thanks. That's a good idea. Giving them to the nurses, that is."

Conway patted Aaron on the shoulder. "By the way, we found that jacket that you were worried about. The ambulance crew had to cut it off him, and they still had it. It's pretty much trashed, but we'll get it back to you when they're done with it in the evidence lab."

Aaron swallowed hard, then choked out, "Oh, yeah," grabbed the flowers from Doris's hands and left as quickly as he'd entered.

CHAPTER 22

"**W**as that young man giving you any grief?" asked Conway, his eyes following Aaron as he left the shop. "He's been threatening a lawsuit at the hospital and throwing his weight around."

Christie arched a brow. "Same here. He was getting in my face at first, and then he started crying when he talked about Cameron maybe not getting well. That's when you walked in."

"Doris gave me a call, so I figured it was a good time to check on things."

"Thanks," said Christie. "He's certainly distraught."

Doris brought two mugs of tea from the back. "It's peppermint. Good for the stomach in stressful situations," she said with a wink.

Christie blew a kiss in Doris's direction. "Thanks, Auntie. I'm convinced you're really a guardian angel masquerading as my aunt."

"Yeah, thanks," said the chief. To Christie, he said, "Have you heard that there's been another threat at the Omega nuclear plant? Nathan called me a while ago."

"Why would Nathan call you? Isn't this like a federal-level problem?"

"Yes, and he wouldn't typically involve the local authorities, but this time, the perp didn't go through the normal channels. He called the plant directly and asked for Conan Starr's personal phone line. The receptionist said he identified himself as one of the reps for their health insurance, so she didn't give it a second thought and put the call through. Except Conan wasn't in at the time, so the message was recorded in his voicemail."

"Will you be able to identify the caller?"

"I called the Feds right away, and they're working on it now. But if it was one of those burner phones, we may not be able to identify anyone."

"What about voice recognition? I've seen that used on television." Christie suppressed a snicker as she tried to picture Chief Conway playing the part of someone on one of the investigative shows.

"Unfortunately, whoever called was using one of those voice-altering devices, like they also use on television."

"Will the FBI get called in?" Christie pictured agents with bulletproof vests swarming in at the Omega plant. "Don't they have technicians who can do some kind of magic and find out who the caller really was?"

Conway shook his head. "Don't know yet. Nathan will decide whether or not to elevate the threat high enough to get those heavyweights involved. Right now, he's not convinced that the call was a credible threat."

"I understand." Christie sat back in her chair. "Was it true what you said about Cameron breathing on his own? That he's off the ventilator?"

"He might be by now," said Conway. "The nurse said they were planning to take the tube out of his lungs sometime this afternoon if he continued to improve. He's following commands, and his vital signs are stable."

"So you were just assuming he's off the ventilator by now?" Christie gave him a look.

"Yeah, I said that to get Aaron out of your face, which was my primary intent."

"Thank you for that." Christie took a long swallow of the warm tea. "Aaron's reaction to your telling him that the jacket was found was interesting. Although maybe it didn't mean anything. I figured he'd be really happy it was found, even if it was trashed."

"Yeah. I don't expect the boys in the evidence lab to learn anything, but Aaron was so intent on finding the thing it made me suspicious."

"When will you know more about it?"

Conway checked his watch. "If this weren't Friday, I'd say tomorrow. But they know it's important, so I might still hear something today, even if it's after hours. They know I want the information before Monday. That's what paying overtime for working after hours and on weekends is for." He chuckled. "Well, I'd better go check on a couple of things before dispatch goes nuts. If Aaron makes a scene at the hospital, I'll have to go there myself because Detective McAvoy has the evening off. It's his anniversary, he said."

"One more question," said Christie. "Did you see the weekly *White Castle Gazette* this morning?"

"It was on my desk when I got to the station. I read it, but I'd take it with a big pinch of salt, Christie. News, good or bad, sells newspapers, and there hasn't been anything else exciting around here during the past week."

"It's not good for business, Conway," Christie said sternly. "Even if you find out what really happened and the paper publishes a corrected story next week, my customers may already be shopping down the road by then."

. . .

Christie and her aunt closed up shop after spiffing up the work area for the next day. Christie was ready to lock the front door when she saw Anita's car pull up. She held the door open for her friend and locked it behind her.

"Hey, Anita. What brings you here on a Friday afternoon?"

"I couldn't wait till this evening to tell you what Nathan said about his and Aaron's Aunt Michelle," said Anita."

Christie groaned and motioned for Anita to follow her. "I doubt I'll ever forget Michelle Starr." She led the way to the back of the shop, retrieving the chair Aaron had been sitting on as they passed the sales counter. She dragged it to the table for Anita. "Have a seat in my consultation office and tell me the big news."

Anita sat with her elbows on the table, her eyes wide. "Nathan says Michelle dropped a big bomb last night and told Conan she was thinking about a divorce."

"While her daughter is on her honeymoon?"

"Yes. Imagine coming home to that kind of news." Anita put her hands to the sides of her head.

"Did she say why? Did she give a reason?"

"She claims it's because of the stress of Conan being the manager of the nuclear plant. And all the drama that goes on with the recent threats and how she's afraid of living so close if the plant blows up or something goes wrong."

"But those aren't new worries, except maybe this latest round of threats. There has to be something else going on, don't you think?"

Anita cocked her head. "The bit about Cameron collapsing and Aaron throwing his weight around, maybe?"

"That has to do with the wedding reception, not the nuclear plant. I can't think of any way in which they could be connected or trigger her to say she wants a divorce."

"I agree with you about that," said Anita, "but all of it is stressful."

Christie sighed. "I feel sorry for Conan, although I barely met him at the end of the reception. And Hailey. Parents splitting up is disturbing, even when the children are adults."

Anita scoffed. "Nathan says Michelle has been a high-maintenance woman all the years he's been around. Even Arthur, Nathan's father, agrees with him, he said."

"Maybe she's just being a drama queen to get the attention focused back on her," said Christie.

Anita smiled. "Now *that* I could believe."

"Going back to the reception for a moment, I have a question for you." Christie leafed through the photos taken by Leanne in the wedding portfolio on the table and found the one with the drink with berries in the glass. "Do you remember seeing this drink on your table? I asked you about it over the phone, but I thought seeing it might trigger your memory."

Anita studied the picture. "Let me think. Nathan had gone over to talk to Aaron. Aaron had waved him over to his table, and when he came back a few minutes later Nathan was carrying that drink. He said it was a peace offering from Michelle."

"Why would she do that?"

"I guess she was trying to smooth things over after Arthur and Doyle got into it at the punch bowl—you know, some gay-bashing that didn't go over well."

"Yeah. I overheard some of that from where I was standing," said Christie. "It looks like Nathan didn't drink it."

Anita nodded and said, "He was drinking Scotch and said he didn't want anything from Michelle or Aaron. So even though Aaron insisted he take it, he told me he wasn't going to drink it. So he let it sit on the table where Michelle could see it."

"And Aaron, too, I would think," said Christie. "Sounds like he was trying to give them a message. We can talk about it more at the Rock tonight."

CHAPTER 23

Christie drove the short distance to The Rock, where she was going to meet the others for a Friday evening meal instead of a movie and drinks they'd talked about earlier in the week. It didn't serve high-quality food necessarily, but pub food was what she craved sometimes, like tonight. Jason had a late-afternoon court appearance with one of his clients and hadn't been sure what time he'd be able to get away, but he'd still managed to beat her to the pub after all. He was holding court at a table on the far side of the room, across from where a trio of musicians—a guitarist, drummer and banjo player—was playing something unrecognizable.

"Where are Nathan and Anita?" Christie asked, as she looked around the room.

Talking loudly over the din, Jason replied, "Nathan got tied up with something at the nuclear plant so I gave him a rain check."

"Okay. I can catch up with Anita later. She was going to tell me something about those drinks at the reception." Christie draped her jacket over the chair and sat next to Jason at the hi-top table. "Did you hear that the jacket Aaron was ranting about showed up?" Christie asked after the waiter took their orders. She told Jason about Aaron showing up at her shop, followed soon thereafter by Chief Conway and the revelation about the jacket. "I swear he started choking when Conway said they'd found it all cut up and that it had been sent to the evidence lab, like he's never going to see it again. Sheesh. How sentimental can he be over a sports coat?"

"I guess we'll know more when Conway gets the report," said Jason. "It's Friday, however, so he probably won't know anything till Monday."

"Not so," replied Christie. "He's asked for a rush job. He was hoping to know something tonight or tomorrow."

"I wonder what he thinks the jacket will tell him." Jason shrugged. "But at least it seems like he's backed off on your flowers being the cause of Cameron's collapse."

"And he's not talking about looking for a murderer anymore." Christie put her elbows on the table, propping up her chin with her hands. "He even came to my rescue at the shop when Aaron came in this morning." Christie related how Conway and McAvoy washed the graffiti from her front window. "Conway figures it was Aaron acting out. Right after that is when Aunt Doris showed me the newspaper with that awful headline. I hope it doesn't hurt my business too badly."

Jason reached across the table and took Christie's hand. "Headlines sell papers, whether it's the truth or not."

"I want to talk to that reporter and give her a piece of my mind," Christie wailed. "She has no right to print allegations like that. Where's her proof?"

"Let Conway do his thing. It will all die down when he figures out where the poison, whatever it was, came from. And how it got into Cameron."

Their server arrived with two pints of draft IPA beer and their food orders.

"Cheers," said Jason, clinking his mug with Christie's. "I'm starved. I didn't get a chance to go out for lunch today because a client needed a letter drafted urgently."

"Do you get to charge him extra for that?" Christie dipped a wing in the rich mahogany-colored sauce and took a bite. "Yum." She licked her fingers.

"How are those buffalo wings, by the way?"

"Messy, but good." Christie wiped the honey barbecue sauce from her chin. "Why in the world do you suppose someone decided to call chicken wings 'buffalo' wings? Wouldn't that be fraud?"

Jason laughed. Christie tended to speak her mind, sometimes too readily, even when it made her sound naïve at times.

"If it bothers you," said Jason, "perhaps you should stick to hamburgers."

"Well, then I'd ask why we call them *ham*burgers when there's no ham in them. They should be called beefburgers instead."

Jason shook his head and took a bite of his halibut fish and chips. "Do you suppose they originated in Hamburg, Germany? Maybe that's why."

Christie threw a wadded-up napkin at him.

Between bites of chicken and swallows of the cold beer, Christie told Jason the news Anita had conveyed about Michelle Starr's divorce bombshell. "That's about all Conan needs right now, with the complaints and threats and all at the nuclear plant. She's got a lousy sense of timing."

Jason muttered, "Uh huh," between bites of french fries.

"That reminds me," said Christie. "There's been another threat at the nuclear plant. Someone called and left a message on Conan's personal landline at work. Chief Conway told me about it. He's helping Nathan because of the urgency of the situation."

Jason nodded. "That's probably what has Nathan tied up tonight. Sounds like the people responsible for the threats are spiraling. Conway might need to take serious action to protect the population."

"Do you mean like an evacuation or calling in the National Guard?"

"Or deactivating the plant." Jason swigged some beer.

Christie's eyes widened. "None of those sound like good options to me. They would all take time. I think finding out who is responsible is the only logical solution."

"I agree. I'm sure Nathan's team is analyzing the most recent email letter and telephone message with all the manpower he has available."

Christie's phone vibrated in her back pocket. "It's Anita," she said after checking the screen. "Maybe she got the answer to my question already."

"What question?"

Christie held up a finger while she answered the phone. "Hi. Did Nathan know about the drink?…Yeah, I'll tell Jason. Talk to you later."

Jason reached across the table to take Christie's hand. "What question? What drink?"

"Remember I told you about a drink on the table where Nathan and Anita were sitting," said Christie, "and it looked like it had berries in it?"

"I think so. What about it?"

"Nathan said Aaron had given it to him, but he was already drinking scotch, so even though he took it, he didn't drink any of it."

"So?" Jason wasn't following her logic.

"We found Cameron on the floor with an empty glass just like it next to him. What if that drink had been poisoned and was meant for Nathan, but Cameron drank it instead?" Christie stabbed a finger in the air.

"Poisoned with what?" asked Jason. "I thought the toxicology studies didn't find a definite poison."

"That's what I understand, but whatever caused Cameron's collapse acted like a poison. But who would put anything in the drink anyway?"

CHAPTER 24

$\mathcal{A}$nita and Nathan were waiting in Nathan's car in front of Christie's house when she arrived home after dinner with Jason. They jumped out of the car, their excitement palpable.

"What's going on? You look like you know something," Christie said as she opened the door. "Is it a good something or a bad something?"

"Let's all sit down, and we'll tell you," said Anita.

"Have a seat in the living room while I open a bottle of wine, and I'll join you in a minute," said Christie.

"I'll help you," said Anita.

Christie quickly placed some cookies on a plate while Anita opened a Cabernet Sauvignon from a local winery. In a matter of minutes, the women placed a tray of wine and glasses plus the cookies on the coffee table in front of Nathan where he sat on the sofa.

"I'll do the honors," said Nathan. He poured the wine while Christie and Anita sat down.

Stormy hopped off her pillow and curled up on Christie's lap, as she sat in her grandma's chair.

After the usual "Cheers," Christie asked, "What's the news? It has to be something major to cause you to come over in person on a Friday night. Jason said you were busy with the nuclear plant. We missed chatting with you at dinner."

Anita said, "Same here. Anyway, I told you earlier that Michelle told Conan she wants a divorce. That happened last night, and that's bad enough, but Nathan found out today that Michelle and Conan got a frantic call from Ryan, their new son-in-law."

"What happened?"

"Nathan, you tell her," said Anita. "You got the information first-hand from your aunt."

Nathan sat with his hand on Anita's knee on the sofa. He cleared his throat. "Hailey was seriously injured when they were snorkeling over a coral reef. She got too close to an underwater shipwreck and cut her leg on a piece of iron sticking out from the hull. The gash was bleeding hard enough that it attracted a couple of sharks before Ryan was able to get her out of the water. Ryan had to fight them off with the help of a couple of other people from the excursion boat. She had lost quite a lot of blood by the time they got her to a hospital in St. Thomas. Aunt Michelle said she needed transfusions and emergency surgery because of the severity of the injury but that it looked like she was going to be okay."

"That's terrible news. Are Michelle and Conan going to fly down to be with her?"

"They didn't know yet," said Nathan. "Ryan apparently told Michelle to stay here, but she's the kind of woman to take charge so she'll probably go anyway. Conan really can't leave right now with the situation at the nuclear plant."

Christie threw her head back. "What a way to end a honeymoon. And then Hailey's parents' divorce on top of it."

The threesome sat quietly together for a few minutes. The clock ticked in the background. Stormy purred on Christie's lap.

Anita shivered involuntarily, and Nathan placed an arm around her shoulders.

"I had a thought earlier today about the poisoning situation," said Christie. "Maybe we're looking at this from the wrong angle. It's hard for me to believe that Cameron was the actual target of any kind of ill will, considering that he was maybe a last-minute guest."

"I agree with you," said Nathan. "And if that's true, there has to be another person who was the real target of the poisoning attempt."

Christie pointed a finger at Nathan. "If the glass on the floor next to Cameron was the same kind of glass that Aaron offered you, it's feasible that *you* were the intended target."

"That's only true if the glass had some kind of poison in it," added Anita. "We still don't know for sure what was in the glass. Or if it was the same one instead of just any glass Cameron knocked over as he fell."

"And why would I be the target in the first place?" asked Nathan. "I wasn't on the guest list originally, as far as I know. I got invited at the last minute when Hailey found out that I was in the area doing the Omega investigation."

Christie shrugged, realizing maybe her newest theory wasn't watertight. "Nathan, maybe you were the poisoner instead, acting out of anger. That makes as much sense as Cameron being a target. Which doesn't make any sense, anyway."

Nathan's eyes widened. "I hope you're teasing because I certainly have no issue with Cameron. And I was fresh out of poison that evening."

The three of them chuckled at the absurdity of the idea.

"Well," said Christie. "*Someone* had it in their pocket."

Anita pulled her legs up under her. "Is there someone who wanted to ruin the wedding for some reason? Like a scorned ex-boyfriend?"

"I doubt it," said Nathan, his hackles settling. "Hailey went to one of those boarding schools back east for high school and Stanford for college. I can't imagine that there were any old boyfriends around here. And if there were, they would be from middle school days."

"Hmm. Michelle isn't exactly the most likable woman," said Christie. "Would that be enough to want to take revenge by ruining her daughter's wedding?"

Anita chuckled. "I think I remember reading that women are more likely to use poison to kill someone instead of more violent means. Like guns."

"Okay," said Christie. "That might be a clue in favor of the suspect being a female."

"But *which* female?" Nathan ran fingers through his dark hair. "It would logically need to be someone who was at the reception."

"Chief Conway has the list," said Christie. "He told Aunt Doris and me that the detective would be interviewing the guests."

"It would take days to track down and personally question every one of them," said Anita. "I'm sure there were at least two hundred people in that church."

Christie groaned. "Well, then that means it will give us more time to find a better suspect for him to consider. Nathan, can you help us find out more about Cameron? We don't know anything about him other than he came as Aaron's guest—and partner if our assumption that they're a couple is correct."

Anita said, "I have a better idea. Remember when Jason used his private detective to help you find Missy and Brian? I'm sure Jason would help you with this."

Christie said, "I like that idea," and grabbed her cell.

Jason picked up on the first ring. "Do you miss me already?" he teased.

"Anita and Nathan are here," replied Christie, hoping her cheeks didn't look pink in the soft light of her living room. "We have an idea that might help Chief Conway find the real culprit."

"I take it the idea involves me somehow," said Jason.

"Yes, and no. It technically involves your private detective." Christie looked up from her cell at Anita and Nathan, who were staring at her, identical expectant looks on their faces.

"And what do you need to have my guy detect?"

"Well, I don't think it would be all that hard. We'd like to know more about Cameron, like what does he do and where does he live and if has any enemies. You know, basic detective stuff."

Jason chuckled. "I know what you mean, Christie. Sure. I'll touch base with him tomorrow and ask him to get started. Is there anyone else you have on your list for detective work?"

Christie said to Anita and Nathan, "Jason will get on it tomorrow. Is there anyone else he should have his guy look into?"

"Maybe Aaron," said Nathan. "He's been pretty cagey with all this. And I don't know much about him even though he's my cousin."

CHAPTER 25

Christie hit the snooze button several times before dragging herself out of bed Saturday morning. She had lain awake until after midnight, her mind going wild with unanswered questions. This was one of the rare mornings when she wished she had a normal job with so-called banker's hours, working nine to five, Monday through Friday. But it was her turn to staff the flower shop. Despite the longer hours involved with owning her own business and the recent stresses with the newspaper stories, she had no interest in working for someone else again. Even if she was promised regular hours and no working on Saturdays and maybe even a bonus at Christmas.

She and Aunt Doris had settled into a routine of taking turns working alternate Saturdays except during busy floral holidays like Mother's Day when they worked side by side. Heather was a helpful assistant most Saturdays as well. She appeared to enjoy the art of creating bouquets and arrangements in addition to her task of doing the deliveries at the end of the day.

The spring flowers were in full bloom now, the weather having warmed up in the second half of April. Christie smiled as she drove by the homes on her way to the shop. The lilacs and azaleas were a blaze of pinks, whites and purples, like a Monet painting. Perhaps one day she would go to Giverny, France, and see Monet's garden in person, she thought wistfully.

She stopped smiling when she stepped in through the back entrance and saw Chief Conway's cruiser parked in front, obviously waiting for her to open for business. She groaned. *What now,* she thought to herself as she lifted Stormy to her perch above the sales counter before walking to the front door to unlock it. She managed to put a thin smile on her face while the chief stepped out of the car. It faded when she saw that Detective McAvoy was with him. She felt her heart flutter when she realized the implications. She stepped aside and closed the door behind them.

"Good morning, gentlemen. What's on your mind?"

Chief Conway shuffled his feet. "I hate to tell you this, Christie, but I got the report from the evidence lab."

"You've sent a lot of evidence to the lab," she replied. "Which report are you referring to?"

"The jacket."

"Cameron's jacket?"

"Of course. The lab found traces of *atropa belladonna* in the breast pocket."

Christie stared at him with narrowed eyes. "And just how would I have anything to do with that? I didn't know Cameron and didn't meet him until after he collapsed at the country club."

"Detective McAvoy thinks you might have put belladonna berries into his pocket after he collapsed. You were the first one to find him, weren't you?"

Christie's mouth dropped open. She took a big breath. "What possible motive would I have to do such a thing? And when and where would I have gotten said berries?"

"That's what we're wondering, Ms. O'Mara," said McAvoy.

"I had no berries and did no such thing. And I wasn't the first one to find Cameron. It was Heather who saw him lying on the floor by the wall. I can't believe you could even imagine she or I would or could do such a thing."

Conway stood with his hands in front of him, holding his hat. "We're trying to come up with a scenario that would explain how traces of belladonna ended up in the jacket. Can you help us with that?"

Christie scoffed. "You should be looking for someone who brought belladonna to the reception. Someone who had a motive because it wasn't me. There never were any belladonna berries in the flower order. You saw it yourself."

McAvoy looked at Conway. "She's right, Chief, about someone else possibly bringing the poison in."

Conway scratched his head. "Christie, maybe you could help us find out how an ordinary person would get belladonna."

Christie crossed her arms and looked at the chief. "Isn't that what detectives do?" She asked without thinking. "Oh, I'm sorry I said that." She tapped a foot, her arms still crossed, eyes looking upward. "Here's a thought to consider. Maybe Cameron brought it. That was his jacket, after all."

Conway stroked his chin. "I just thought of something else. Aaron was ranting and raving about needing to find the jacket. Maybe he knew there was belladonna in the pocket and didn't want us to find it."

"That's right," said Christie. "And in retrospect, he didn't seem relieved to find out you sent it to the evidence lab instead of giving it directly to him. I thought he was choked up because he was sentimental about the stupid jacket, but maybe it was guilt."

Conway and McAvoy looked at each other, faces grim.

"McAvoy, let's go talk to Aaron Starr," said Conway. "And ask him about the jacket."

"That sounds like a marvelous idea," said Christie. "I really do want you to find the person responsible for all this, but right now, I have a business to run. At least for the moment."

Heather had arrived for work while Christie was talking to Conway and McAvoy. Once they were out the door, she approached Christie and said, "I overheard Chief Conway saying something about traces of belladonna and suspecting it came from berries. But what about seeds? Would they be just as poisonous? I bet you could check online and see if you can buy them in the same way my mom buys seeds for her vegetable garden."

Christie high-fived her smart assistant. "What a wonderful idea, Heather. Let's boot up the computer and find out."

It took less than five minutes to find several online sources for seeds and berries of *Atropa belladonna* from various nurseries and even liquid forms from chemical companies. She was shocked to discover that she, or anybody, could purchase a packet of thirty seeds for less than five dollars. Christie printed a list to give to the detective and called him to relay the information.

She felt a little more optimistic for the first time in the week since Cameron's collapse. Being able to prove that someone could easily purchase the seeds wasn't the same as identifying the person who did it, but it did prove that someone other than a florist had access to belladonna, albeit in another form.

CHAPTER 26

After McAvoy came by to pick up the list, Christie and Heather worked together on an arrangement of happy yellow chrysanthemums, sassy pink carnations, and snowy white roses that was to be delivered for a sixteenth birthday party that afternoon. Christie explained the process of selecting the proper vase and the order in which to place the stems of flowers and greens to create the final, beautiful product.

She watched Heather deftly insert stems of pale gray-green eucalyptus and narrow dracaena spires into the tall, narrow vase, smiling as she admired the results.

"It seems easier to do after your explanation," said Heather. "I hope I can take a class this summer and learn more. My mom said I could even drive to Vancouver if I wanted to and if you gave me some time off."

"Sounds like a great idea. I think you have a natural talent for it."

Heather beamed. "It's fun."

While Heather prepared the vase for transportation, Christie tackled the order list she would call in Monday morning. She had learned to wait until after the weekend to make the call.

More often than not, a death on Friday or Saturday triggered a flurry of calls on Monday for flowers for the bereaved. She liked the boost in her business but always felt sad for the ones left behind.

The front door chimed. She looked up from her desk to see Jason enter with Nathan. They both had sly smiles on their faces.

"You look like you have secrets to tell," said Christie.

Jason said, "My PI dug up some interesting information about Cameron and Aaron."

"And I," said Nathan, "did more research on the source of the last round of threats at Omega. Meanwhile, the NRC received a threat from the same computer targeting the nuclear plant near Palo Verde."

"And would you like to guess where Aaron and Cameron live?" asked Jason with a grin from ear to ear.

Christie took the bait. "Would it be Palo Verde?"

"No," said Jason, "but very close. Palo Verde has three operating nuclear stations about fifty miles west of Phoenix. They have spent the last two years living in Goodyear, Arizona."

"Never heard of it. Why is that important?"

"Goodyear is about forty miles from Palo Verde," replied Jason. "There's an active anti-nuclear group in the region that Ben, my investigator, was able to tap into. He found Aaron's and Cameron's names in some of the documents that were on the website."

"Are you suggesting that they might be behind the complaints filed against Omega?" Christie asked, aghast with the revelation. "But Aaron's uncle is the manager there. That doesn't make sense."

"Frankly, very little of what those organizations do makes sense to logical people," said Nathan. "My IT team is still trying to determine the ISP identification of the computer involved, but my bet is that it's going to link back to Aaron."

"That still doesn't tell us why Cameron was poisoned or if he was the intended target," said Christie. "I can't believe that Aaron would be connected to that."

"Like Nathan said, anti-nuclear people do unexpected things," Jason iterated.

"I have some news, too," said Christie. "Conway and McAvoy came by this morning to tell me that the missing jacket, now found, had traces of belladonna in the breast pocket. It was the same jacket Aaron had been so frantic to find. They were on their way to talk to Aaron when they left here."

"Hmm," said Jason. "He definitely has some explaining to do."

Nathan said, "I'd love to see him squirm his way out of that one."

"Conway's still not letting me off the hook, though," said Christie. "He had the gall to ask me if I knew where to buy belladonna berries! As if I'd tell him even if I did know. But Heather suggested we look online, and we found out it would be easy for anyone to buy belladonna in several forms, including seeds and liquid."

Jason nodded and said, "Didn't the article in Wikipedia that Anita read to us say that all parts of the plant are poisonous, but to different degrees?"

"Seeds would be less messy than fresh berries in a jacket pocket as well. I would assume that either form could leave traces behind," suggested Christie.

"Even if I come up with a logical reason that Cameron would carry poison in the first place," said Nathan, "it makes no sense that he would end up poisoning himself. Unless it was a mistake somehow. But maybe he was carrying it for Aaron to use to poison someone, maybe even me. I mean, they were apparently both anti-nuclear energy, and he did accuse me of pandering to Uncle Conan and turning a blind eye if I even found a problem while investigating Omega. But, again, he didn't know I would be there unless he found out from Hailey just before the wedding. He wouldn't have had time to order anything online if he didn't know about my being there until the last minute."

"You're forgetting about Amazon Prime," said Christie. "I've had items delivered the same day."

"Since I don't use that service," said Nathan, "I wouldn't know how fast they can deliver orders. But same-day delivery might be the answer, assuming that the closest warehouse keeps said item in stock."

"And if not you, then who else might have been the real target?" asked Christie. "And why?"

"I don't know who or why,' said Nathan, "but Aaron's connection to the anti-nuclear group in Goodyear is worrisome. I worry that something major is brewing. The recent direct call to Uncle Conan has the NRC on edge. My director said he's on the verge of bringing in the National Guard in case we have to order an evacuation of everyone within thirty miles of Omega. That would include White Castle, of course."

"I'm beginning to understand why nuclear plants are usually built far away from major cities," said Christie. "But wouldn't it be more logical and faster to simply disable the plant's nuclear power generator?"

Nathan pressed his lips together. "In theory, yes, but it's not like you can simply pull a plug. It's quite a complicated process, although it would spare the population the stress of a full evacuation."

"And I'm sure the NRC is doing everything it can to identify the source of the threats to avoid either scenario," said Jason. "Is that correct, Nathan?"

"The last thing anyone wants is a nuclear leak or unnecessary panic in the community. Most people don't know that there are about ninety active nuclear stations around the country. The typical person knows about the disasters at Chernobyl and Three Mile Island but is generally unaware of the overall safety of nuclear plants or where they are unless they happen to live in a community like White Castle."

"Yeah," said Christie. "We just go blissfully along with our normal lives until something unusual occurs to remind us of our nuclear neighbor." She looked at Nathan, whose face seemed to have suddenly developed new worry lines. "Are you worried about an immediate threat of something serious happening at Omega?"

Nathan looked down, avoiding her eyes, and just replied, "I really can't discuss it."

$\mathcal{A}$aron burst into Christie's shop just before noon. She had looked up to see who had triggered the door chime and, seeing who it was, she stood, steeled her spine and met him halfway. She slowed her steps when she realized he looked more frightened than angry.

"Hi, Aaron. What's wrong? How can I help you today?"

"Christie, I need to apologize for being such a pigheaded moron earlier, but now I need your help." Aaron's hands shook, and it wasn't because of cold. The mid-day April temperature was seventy-four degrees, according to the outdoor thermometer on the bank across the street.

"I'm not sure how I could possibly help you, but what's the problem?"

"The police chief, Conway, is asking questions about how traces of belladonna got into Cameron's jacket pocket. He implied that I might have poisoned Cameron myself." Aaron's whole body started trembling. "You have to know I would never do anything like that."

"I tend to believe you, but I don't understand what kind of help I might be able to provide." Christie smiled wryly.

"He even said he didn't need much more evidence to prove I was definitely guilty."

Christie cocked her head. "Chief Conway has to ask questions of everyone who might be connected to Cameron and the jacket, I suppose. That doesn't mean he thinks you're guilty."

"You didn't hear the tone of voice he used when he asked me about the jacket."

Christie pointed to her consultation table and started walking in that direction. "Come on back, and I'll make you a cup of tea. You can tell me more about it."

Aaron sat at the table, his fingers tapping on the wooden surface, his eyes darting around the room. "How do you put the flowers together so they look so beautiful?" He pointed at the floral bouquets in the cooler. "That must take a lot of talent."

Christie set the mugs of peppermint tea on the table and sat down across from her guest. "I learned from my grandma, who opened this shop thirty years ago or so, and Aunt Doris, who still works here."

"Is that the older lady with the frizzy red hair?"

"That's the one. She's very good with design and making something out of practically anything. Back when I was in high school and college, I worked for her during the summers. Grandma paid for me to take a few classes in specialty techniques, like ikebana. That's an elegant form of flower arrangement that originated with the Japanese."

"You're good at it." Aaron sipped the tea and nibbled on a biscotti that Christie had put on a small plate in front of him. "Thanks. This is delicious."

"If you didn't poison your friend Cameron, who do you think did? And how? And why *were* there traces of belladonna in his jacket?"

"I swear I wouldn't hurt Cameron. We're planning on getting married eventually. I think. Anyway, I guess it couldn't really be your flowers after all. I mean, that would require him to have eaten them somehow, and that doesn't make sense."

"I agree with you there." She didn't feel the need to point out that the poison was from another plant altogether since he had already taken her off his suspect list. "Here's another question for you. What was in the drink that you offered Nathan at the reception? I saw pictures of the glass on the table and it looked like it had berries in it."

Aaron wrinkled his face. "I don't remember what was in it, but I know it was a spiked punch of some kind. Aunt Michelle was serving it from the punch bowls across from the main bar at the club. She explained that there were blueberries in the bottom of the glasses of alcoholic punch and nothing in the other glasses so we could tell them apart. After a little, well, let's say, unhappy moment with the family, she insisted I take three glasses, two of the spiked punch and one for Cameron without berries. She wanted me to try to make amends with Nathan. I was going, you know, to thank him, even if belatedly, for standing up for me when my Uncle Arthur was hammering on gays."

"I understand you weren't close with your family," said Christie.

"That's true, unfortunately." Aaron looked at his feet, then met Christie's eyes. "My dad, Doyle, the youngest of the Starr brothers, drilled it into my head all my life that Uncle Conan couldn't be trusted. And neither could his corrupt son Nathan. But I wanted to at least shake hands and see if we could have a decent relationship without dragging our fathers into it. I admit I was quite shocked when I first found out that Nathan was investigating our uncle's nuclear plant. How can he do that impartially?" He scoffed. "It was more than suspicious to me that he'd be the one to volunteer to work this case. He lives in Texas, after all, and that's a long way from Washington state. Then I found out that he was going to be at the wedding."

Christie swallowed back that Nathan said he'd actually been enlisted to do the investigation because no one else was readily available. "So what happened at the reception that had your aunt wanting you three to make amends?" Christie had heard the argument but wanted Aaron's view of it.

"Several of us had been at the bar just before that. Nathan's dad, who *is* openly homophobic, said something derogatory about gays. My dad said nothing in return. Nathan tried to defend me, I guess, to our dads, but I'd had enough and left for the punch table. Uncle Arthur insisted on getting another drink from the open bar when Aunt Michelle wouldn't serve him. So when I got to the punch table, Aunt Michelle, who had heard the whole thing, suggested I not let the evening end with us mad at each other. That's why I took the punch glasses for Nathan and me, as well as one for Cameron. I went over to Nathan and invited him over to meet Cameron. I was a little surprised that he agreed to join us. I offered the glass to him, you know, like a peace offering, and he took a couple of swallows, and we shook hands before he went back to his girlfriend. A few minutes later, I went outside and asked to have my car brought around so Cameron and I could leave."

Christie grabbed her phone and found the photo with the drink. "Is this like the one you gave to Nathan?"

Aaron peered at the screen, enlarging it for detail. "It looks like it. Why?"

"Those might be belladonna berries. The bad kind."

"Are you suggesting that my aunt might have been the culprit here? She told me they were blueberries so I could tell which of the glasses were spiked. The non-alcoholic punch didn't have any berries. You know, it was plain, just a pink-colored punch."

Christie nodded slowly. "I heard that she wasn't thrilled that you were going to be one of the groomsmen, especially when you came with Cameron."

"Yeah. She's been pretty cold to me, but Hailey and Ryan asked me, and they said they had the final say on the invitation list. I understand my dad wasn't initially invited either—he and Uncle Conan don't like each other much. Dad said it goes back to him hating Conan for stealing Michelle from him. But that was in high school. Anyway, he said it wasn't any of my business about his not being invited. But I was glad to see him sitting in the back of the church and at the reception." Aaron smiled. "I guess he had a change of heart and decided not to let Aunt Michelle tell him what to do."

Aaron sat back in the chair, hands between his knees, head hanging forward for a moment. He sighed and looked up. "If what you say is true, and those are belladonna berries, Aunt Michelle handed me a poisoned drink? For who? Me or Nathan?" He shook his head, looking as confused as Christie felt.

Christie nodded grimly. "Did you tell all this to Chief Conway? He'll want to interview her."

"No, we only talked about the jacket, not about any drinks."

"Well, you need to tell him about Michelle handing you those three drinks."

Aaron's cell played a short tune, and he pulled it from his back pocket. After reading the message, he said, "Cameron's starting to remember what happened. He wants me to come see him." He swallowed the rest of his tea and stood to leave.

Christie had a couple more questions but didn't want to get in the way of Aaron's going to the hospital to see his friend. She was completely bamboozled that the angry Aaron had been replaced by this new person. She glanced at the time. It was almost time to close anyway, with her shorter Saturday hours. "Would you mind if I go with you? I'd love to meet Cameron now that he's able to talk."

Aaron hesitated a few beats before saying, "I think that would be okay."

"Let me send Heather out for the deliveries, and I'll close up the store and join you in about thirty minutes."

Aaron offered a hand, which was no longer trembling. "See you there. He's been transferred to the fourth floor, by the way."

CHAPTER 28

*C*hristie quickly called Jason to tell him about Aaron's change of attitude and that she was going to meet him at the hospital to visit Cameron.

"Are you sure that's a good idea? He's been extremely hostile toward you."

"I know," said Christie. "I'm not sure how to reconcile this nicer person with the angry young man of yesterday. But, yeah, I do want to go visit Cameron and ask him some questions on my own."

Jason was quiet for a moment. "What about Chief Conway? Are you going to tell him?"

"I thought about it, but I don't want to jeopardize this opportunity with Aaron. I don't know what he'd be like if Conway were there also."

"I agree with you there, Christie, but you will tell him afterward, won't you?"

"Yes, of course, I will. Conway will want to talk to him anyway. I'm just getting a head start."

"Understood. Call me later."

Christie locked her business's back door and opened the

passenger door of her SUV. As she helped Stormy into her cat carrier, she said, "You'll have to wait in the car while I make a quick stop at St. Joseph Hospital. I promise I won't take long. Maybe Cameron will be able to fill in some of the missing pieces."

~

FIFTEEN MINUTES LATER, Christie was at the fourth-floor nurses' station asking for Cameron Collins's room number. She was waiting for the secretary to give her the information when she heard Aaron call her name from down the hall. He motioned for her to join him.

"Thank you, Miss," she said to the young lady. "My friend's waving at me, so I know where he is now." Christie hurried down the hall with the smell of antiseptic solutions stinging her nose along the way. She wondered how long it took for those who worked at the hospital to become accustomed to the smell. Or if they ever did.

"Hi, Aaron. How is Cameron?"

"I haven't gotten to talk with him yet but the nurse just finished with him and told me I can go in for a few minutes."

She followed Aaron into the private room. Sunlight streamed into the stark room through the slats of the blinds on the west-facing windows, creating narrow bands of light on the blue bedcovers. Cameron lay in bed, face pale, eyes closed.

Aaron gently touched Cameron's arm, and his eyes popped open. He smiled lovingly at Aaron before turning his head to where Christie stood next to him.

He looked at Aaron and asked, "Who's your pretty friend? Do I know her?"

"I don't think so," replied Aaron. "We didn't get a chance to meet her until the end of the reception."

"I don't remember meeting her. I wouldn't forget a pretty

face like that." He smiled again and said to Christie, "Hi. I'm Cameron. Who are you?"

"Hi, Cameron. I'm Christie. I was in charge of the flowers for Hailey and Ryan's wedding."

"They were beautiful. But how do you know Aaron?"

Aaron and Christie shared a look before Aaron answered for her. "She found you on the floor at the reception. You had a reaction of some kind and had to go to the hospital."

"A reaction? What kind of reaction?"

"Nobody's sure yet," Aaron replied. "The police are still checking on it."

"Do you mean like low blood sugar or something? But I'm not diabetic."

Aaron shook his head. "Doesn't look like that."

Christie jumped in, eager to learn more about Cameron's medical history, which didn't seem to include diabetes at this point. "The police chief is wondering if you had a medication reaction of some kind. Do you take any kind of regular medicine?"

Cameron looked at Aaron. "I don't remember. Do I?"

Aaron smiled grimly, glancing at Christie before he replied. "Yes, for your anxiety. But it's a very small dose and isn't a problem. And you were taking something for a cold before we came to the wedding."

"Do you remember what medicine that was?" Christie asked Cameron as she tried to recall the names of some of the medications that could cause a reaction similar to his.

Cameron shook his head. "My brain is too foggy," he said. Then his face brightened. "But Aaron can tell you. My medication is in my ditty bag at the hotel. He can find it and tell you." He turned and looked at Aaron with an innocent smile. "Can you do that, please? I want to know what happened to me."

Aaron's eyes widened momentarily. "Of course, I'll do that.

I'll find your medicine and let Christie and the police chief know the name of it."

"Thank you. You're good to me. I'm tired, Aaron." Cameron closed his eyes.

The nurse who had been standing just outside the door stepped into the room and said, "He needs his rest. Thank you for leaving." The forced smile didn't get past her lips.

Aaron kissed Cameron on the forehead and squeezed his hand before turning to leave. Christie waited silently at the door for him.

They walked quietly to the elevator, neither of them speaking. When they reached the level of the parking garage, Christie said, "His memory seems to be a little hazy."

Aaron's eyes teared up. He sniffled and blew his nose with a tissue he pulled from his jacket pocket. "The doctors aren't sure how much memory he will regain, but they said it's too early to tell."

"Are you going to find his medication and tell the doctors and Chief Conway what he was taking?" asked Christie. "It might be important for them to know in case there is something they can prescribe that will help him recover more completely."

Aaron sighed heavily and looked Christie in the eye. "Yes, I'll do that. I really didn't think it was important until now. It didn't occur to me that the medications he was taking could be involved in his being sick. I thought he was having a reaction from something at the wedding reception. Like the food or maybe even the flowers."

Christie snorted. "Aaron! Unless he nibbled on a leaf or a flower bud, it would be unlikely that the flowers could be the cause of the problem."

Aaron reddened. "Of course, you're right about that. I know he takes something for anxiety, but I think it's mostly because of having to deal with my family. My own father has made it clear that he won't accept Cameron because he's gay. He seems sure that if Cameron disappeared from my life, I'd go back to being 'normal.'" Aaron scoffed. "He doesn't get it. And I know Aunt Michelle wasn't happy that Hailey and Ryan asked me to be a groomsman. She and my dad aren't close at all, and Uncle Conan is too soft to stand up to her or to defend his own daughter's choices."

"It must have been pretty tough to get through all that," said Christie.

Aaron nodded. "Initially, it was only going to be a couple of days that we had to put up with all that garbage, but then Cameron got sick, and we got stuck here for a while longer. I feel terrible because I talked him into coming to the wedding partly to prove to Aunt Michelle and Uncle Conan that we do normal things and that being gay isn't a disease." Aaron shook his head. "Now I wish we hadn't come."

Christie reached out and put a hand on his arm. "I'm sorry your family has made it hard for you. But what about Cameron's family? You haven't mentioned them." She scanned the lot for her car.

"They kicked him out when he was still in high school after he told them he was gay. I'm all he's got."

Christie spotted her car and pointed to it. "My car's on the far side." She started to cross the center lane of parked cars but stopped and turned instead. "I just remembered something I was going to ask you. I heard you were late getting to the church for the pictures before the wedding. Was that because of Cameron?"

"Uh…No...Um…Aunt Michelle asked me to pick up a package for her at the UPS pickup site. Why?"

"Do you remember anything about the package?"

Aaron wrinkled his face. "It was just one of those brown manila paper things."

"How big?"

"Not very. Like the next size down from a piece of paper."

"You mean copy paper?"

"Yeah. Smaller than that. Why are you so interested in that package?"

Christie shrugged. "It's curious that Michelle wanted it so badly before the wedding that she sent you to get it."

Aaron paled.

CHAPTER 29

*C*hristie rummaged in her refrigerator and found the leftover lasagna her mom had left for her a couple of days earlier. She was grateful that Maureen delivered homemade food, often on Thursdays, while Christie was at her shop. It was handy for a quick lunch or dinner. And was much better than the deli counter at the grocery store or frozen meals.

After the delicious meal, Christie curled up in her favorite chair with Stormy in her lap. She wondered if Aaron had followed through in finding the medicine and what it might have been. She didn't really expect Aaron to call her, nor did he have her personal number anyway. But she certainly wanted to know if it was one of those medications or a combination that could cause belladonna-like symptoms.

Stormy purred in Christie's lap and stretched her head up to nuzzle against her chin. When the doorbell rang, the cat jumped off her lap and headed for the door. Christie got there first and held her foot in front of the cat while opening the door only a few inches to keep Stormy from escaping for an unauthorized mouse hunt.

"Chief Conway!" Surprised, Christie swooped up her cat and

pointed to the living room with her free hand. "Come on in and have a seat. I'll make some tea if you have time. Is Earl Gray okay with you?"

"Sure, if you have cream and sugar."

A few minutes later, Christie set two steaming mugs and a plate of oatmeal raisin cookies on the coffee table in front of the sofa where Conway was sitting. She sat in the chair across from him, her legs curled under her. "You must have some important news to come to my home on a Saturday."

"Your shop was closed when I drove by a while ago, so I took a chance on finding you at home." He took a sip of the tea after doctoring it with half-and-half and several teaspoonfuls of sugar. "Perfect."

Christie drank her tea au naturel. She grimaced when she saw how much sugar Conway added.

"I close up early every other Saturday. That was Aunt Doris's advice from her years of working with my grandma. So, what have you learned, Chief?"

"I'm sure you remember that Aaron Starr has been pretty close-mouthed about his friend, Cameron."

"Yes, and I know it has maybe hindered your investigation."

"Yeah, so I was surprised when he called a half hour ago to tell me that Cameron had been taking some kind of medication for anxiety. He said he thought he should tell me in case it would help Cameron's recovery."

Christie's heart leapt. Her advice to Aaron appeared to have worked. "That sounds like a breakthrough."

"I thought so too, but Aaron couldn't find the medicine in Cameron's belongings, and he said that Cameron couldn't remember the name when he asked, so we're still up that proverbial creek."

Christie's heart thunked. "Did you suggest that he call Cameron's pharmacy or doctor and have them look it up?"

"I did, but he might run into those privacy laws when he tries to find out. And it's a Saturday so that makes the chance of his being able to find out from the doctor directly less likely." Conway banged his fist on the soft cushion of the sofa. "Dang. I thought we were going to get some answers, but we still don't know for sure if there was a medication interaction causing Cameron's problems."

"Can't you get around the privacy laws as a police officer, considering there might be an attempted murder involved?"

"Could, but I hope to find out directly. Aaron said he'd call me later this afternoon. He was going to check with the pharmacy and the doctor on call. He also said you were with him at the hospital."

Christie looked up to the ceiling, feeling a wee bit guilty for not keeping Conway in the loop on that. A change in subject might be in order. "Did Aaron tell you why he was late arriving for the wedding pictures?"

"Is it relevant?"

"Maybe."

"Tell me what you know, then."

Christie reported what Nathan had said about Michelle defending Aaron being late. "I asked Aaron about it because I was curious. Aaron said she asked him to pick up a package at a UPS pick-up site and that she had to have it before the wedding."

"I don't suppose you asked him what was in the package," Conway said snidely.

"I didn't, but I asked him a couple of questions about its size and where it came from, but he didn't recall all the details. Maybe you should ask Michelle Starr about it."

"Hmm. Maybe I should." Conway pulled a small notepad from his shirt pocket and jotted a note.

"Maybe it was an order of belladonna seeds," said Christie.

"Or maybe it was an innocent package of something she needed for the wedding," replied Conway.

Christie snorted. "I'm just pointing out that there are other sources of belladonna, such as ordering over the internet. On another note, Nathan Starr told me about the animosity between Aaron's dad, Doyle, and his uncle Conan, father of the bride and manager of the Omega plant. What about that?"

"First place, this didn't involve Conan Starr."

"Not directly, but it was his daughter's wedding."

"Second place, Cameron Collins isn't related to Mr. Starr."

"But he's a significant other of Aaron, who *is* related to Mr. Starr."

"You're grasping at straws, Christie. It occurs to me that maybe you and Aaron were conspiring when you talked at the hospital earlier."

Christie choked on her tea. "What? Conspire? I barely know the man."

"So you say. I hope I don't find out differently."

"And why would I put my business at risk? What could my motive possibly be?"

Conway raised a brow and slurped a mouthful of tea. His phone vibrated on the table. He glanced at the phone's face and frowned before picking it up and saying, "Conway here." He stood and turned his back toward Christie. A moment later, he said, "On my way."

He bent to pick up his hat from the couch. "Thanks for the tea. And cookies."

Christie followed him to the door. "Where do you have to go?"

Conway narrowed his eyes, plopped his hat on his head, and said, "Can't tell you. Police matter."

Christie closed the door behind him and leaned her back against the closed door, sighing. She asked Stormy, "And why would I conspire to do something like poison someone when all I want to do is sell flowers?"

Stormy looked up from her cat bed and meowed.

CHAPTER 30

$\mathcal{C}$hristie stewed for a few minutes after Conway left. She paced the living room. Something about the package that Aaron picked up for his aunt was important enough to take the risk of interfering with the family wedding photos. She couldn't ask Aaron any more about it. He presumably told her everything he knew and she didn't want to raise his suspicion. Who else might know? Someone she could ask safely, that is, without getting her head bit off.

She stopped in her tracks. "I could ask Nathan," she said aloud, startling Stormy, who looked up from her cozy cat bed. "He's the one who mentioned Aaron having been late in the first place. He might not know anything. But I won't know unless I ask."

Seconds later, she was on her phone calling Anita, who might or might not be with Nathan at the moment but would have his number one way or the other.

"Hi, Anita. You wouldn't happen to be with Nathan right now, would you?"

"No, but I'm fine. And you?"

Christie reddened. "Oh, sorry, my friend. I was so excited

about wanting to ask Nathan a question that I forgot my manners. And I'm fine too, I think."

"What's the question? Or is it for Nathan's ears only?"

"It's not a secret-type question. It's about the reason Aaron was late for the pictures the morning of the wedding."

Anita asked, "I wasn't with him at the time, but what's the question anyway?"

"Well, he mentioned at our Wednesday taco night that Hailey was almost in tears because of Aaron's lateness, him being a groomsman and all, and that his aunt Michelle brushed it off. Nathan said Michelle made some comment about Aaron having to run an errand. At the time Nathan said that, I assumed that meant he had his own errand to run. But Aaron told me Michelle had asked him to pick up a package for her. I wanted to ask Nathan exactly how Michelle worded that—if she could have meant Aaron was on an errand for her or really stated it was his own errand. I'm hoping he recalls."

"Yes, it could be important to know who the package was for," said Anita. "I wonder what was in it? Wait…when did Aaron tell you this, anyway?"

"You're not going to believe this," said Christie, "but Aaron allowed me to meet him at the hospital with him earlier today. He got a call while he was at my shop that Cameron was more awake. When he said he was on his way to visit, I asked if I could join him. I was shocked when he said 'Okay.'"

"You're right, Christie. That's a surprise. So Aaron wasn't accusing you again?"

"Oh, no, he was surprisingly pleasant to me and so despondent about Cameron."

"Hmm, I'd be careful about him, Christie. But back to that package. Clearly, *someone* ordered something, and it was in a small package. Maybe it was a packet of belladonna seeds?" Christie had told her friend what she'd researched about the ease of ordering various forms of belladonna.

"Hmm," said Anita. "I've certainly heard that women tend to use poison for murders, so I suppose it could make sense. But why bring another person into it and risk detection? And what does this have to do with Nathan?" Christie heard a small defensive tone. She realized Anita was getting frustrated that her boyfriend was being accused of anything.

Christie spoke softly into the phone. "I was only hoping he might have seen the envelope himself and have more ideas of what might have been in it."

Anita sighed. "Of course. And maybe he will. I'll text you his contact information, and you can ask him yourself. He mentioned earlier that he was going to call Jason and see about us four getting together for dinner this evening. Have you heard from Jason?"

"Not yet, but it's still early afternoon. Thanks. I can wait and ask Nathan about the package at dinner. Talk to you later."

JASON CALLED while Christie was pruning the roses in her backyard. She hadn't gotten around to doing it earlier in the spring and hoped it wasn't too late to shape the old bushes for the best possible blooms later in the summer. She was grateful for the perfect weather on a Saturday for the task, with Pacific Northwest spring weather being on the fickle side. It could be seventy-five degrees and dry one day and fifty-five and rainy the next. She felt fortunate to have found her small house with mature landscaping, especially with shrubs that she could use in floral arrangements at her shop. And she loved roses but hadn't known the intricacies of taking care of them until doing some reading a few weeks earlier. The cost of the roses she ordered for her business now made a lot of sense.

"Hey. If you're calling to invite me out for dinner, you're too late," said Christie, a twinkle in her eye that Jason couldn't see over the phone.

A pause. "Are you…busy?"

Christie giggled, unable to maintain her composure for more than a few seconds. "Anita spilled the beans earlier when we talked. Although…" She hesitated. Was she starting to take their relationship too much for granted? "…maybe you're calling about something else. Are you?"

"No, I'm calling to see if you want to join Anita and Nathan for dinner at Teri's at the new location on Main Street downtown."

"Sounds lovely. I'd love to. On another note, do you have anything new on Aaron or Cameron?"

"Well, maybe. Don't you want to wait till I see you tonight?"

"Of course not. We might get busy talking about something else, and you won't remember to tell me. What do you know?"

"Ben, my investigator, uncovered emails that Aaron sent to his dad, Doyle, the youngest of the Starr brothers."

"I remember the Starr brothers and something about a rift between a couple of them. Is that what you mean?"

"Yes, there were bad feelings between Aaron's dad, Doyle, and Hailey's dad, Conan. They both had a crush on Michelle in high school days. Remember, they were only two years apart in age, and Michelle was in Doyle's class, two years behind Conan."

"Yeah. So what?"

"Michelle broke up with Doyle, who was her same age, and started dating Conan instead. He was the football captain, and she was the pretty lead cheerleader. Of course, Doyle was pretty angry. The brothers were quite competitive, I understand. Get the picture?"

"I guess so. What happened after that?"

"Well," Jason continued, "Michelle has a cousin, Roxanne,

who ended up dating and marrying Doyle. I guess Doyle got over Michelle by marrying her cousin instead."

"So Doyle married Michelle's cousin after Michelle left him. And Doyle and her cousin Roxanne had Aaron. Right?"

"Yes. And Ben has tracked Doyle to Ionia."

"Ionia? But that's only fifteen miles down the road."

"Yes. He apparently spends winters in Palm Desert and the rest of the time here."

"It seems cold-hearted to exclude him from the wedding when he lives so close. Do you know if that's true?"

"That's a very good question, and I think I'll let Chief Conway handle it from here. I'm calling him when I get off the phone. I'll pick you up at six thirty."

"But I want to know about the emails from Aaron to his dad. What's that got to do with the other two brothers and their marriages?"

"Later, Christie."

CHAPTER 31

Nathan and Anita were already enjoying a glass of wine when Christie and Jason arrived at the restaurant. Their heads were close together as they laughed, apparently enjoying something they found to be funny. The restaurant was full of happy diners, as was typical for the popular eatery on a Saturday night.

"Hey. Sorry to interrupt your conversation," said Christie as they approached the table. She noted that Anita's face had turned red, causing her to wonder what Nathan might have said. "Are you two solving the world's problems?"

Nathan stood and waited for Christie to be seated by Jason. "Not exactly," said Nathan, "but I do have some news about the origin of some of the emails to the Omega nuclear plant."

"Are they from Aaron?" Christie asked, sure he was guilty of something.

"Yes and no."

"Huh? You can't have it both ways."

Nathan grinned slyly. "Actually, I sorta can. The IT guys have verified that several of the emails have Aaron's 'signature,' so to speak, but the source doesn't appear to be connected to him directly."

"Explain, please," said Christie. "I don't talk computer language."

"I'm not going to try to explain the whole process because even I don't understand it, but IT specialists use various tools to trace emails backward to an origin. However, there are dozens of ways that emails can be encrypted and rerouted through channels such as the dark web that make it virtually impossible to identify the original source. Spammers and underground users have become much more sophisticated in their use of these alternative channels, and even the federal government, despite its resources, has difficulty untangling the trails. And that includes the Nuclear Regulatory Commission."

"In other words," said Christie, "you don't know for sure where they're coming from."

"Not yet, but we do think Aaron is somehow involved."

"What if someone else is sending them and making it look like Aaron is the guilty party?" asked Christie. "Can that be done?"

"Of course. And maybe that's what's going on, but we can't prove it. Yet."

"How would that be determined?"

Jason asked, "Are you softening your stance about Aaron? You've been adamant all along that he's guilty of something."

Christie tilted her head and replied, "Maybe guilty of something, but now I'm not so sure that he's responsible for the emails to the nuclear plant or for Cameron's illness. And Nathan just said that the emails could be coming from anywhere."

"Who else might have wanted to hurt Cameron?" asked Anita.

"I'm kinda thinking it might be Michelle," said Christie, "considering how cool she had been toward Aaron, but that doesn't fit with her asking him to pick up the package before the wedding." She turned toward Nathan. "You said before that Michelle defended his lateness. What did she actually say? Do you recall her actual words?"

Nathan frowned. "Hmm. 'Aaron had to run an errand.' I'm pretty sure that was it."

"So, not who the errand was for?"

"No. I mean, I assumed it was something he needed. Why?"

"Aaron told me it was an errand to pick up something for her. Did you see the package that Aaron brought back, and if he gave it to her? Can you describe it, as in how big and how thick, or did you see where it came from?"

"I didn't see it," said Nathan. "That must have happened outside the church, and I was inside with the other family members."

"So not very helpful," Christie bemoaned.

"What do you mean?" asked Nathan. "What did you want it to contain?"

Christie shrugged. "The belladonna in some form, like seeds, maybe, that could be added to a drink. Aaron told me that there were two kinds of punch near the bar. One bowl was spiked, and one wasn't. Michelle served the spiked punch in glasses with blueberries so as to tell it from the plain punch in the plain glasses."

"But that doesn't make sense," said Anita. "How could she add belladonna to the plain punch if it was in the form of seeds? They'd probably be floating or sitting in the bottom of the glass."

"You're right," said Christie, deflated. "Back to square one."

"And why would Michelle want Aaron or Nathan to be poisoned in the first place if that's what happened?"

Nathan interrupted with, "Let's eat, drink and be merry. No more wedding or poison talk for now."

The waitress brought two additional wine glasses for Christie and Jason and took the dinner orders. Nathan poured wine all around. "No belladonna in this drink," he announced as the four raised their glasses in a toast to friendship.

Christie shared her conversation with Aaron and Cameron at the hospital. "Aaron seems more friendly to me for now, but I don't trust him just yet. I wish we could prove somehow that there was another way his partner became ill."

"You mentioned that Cameron was on some medications prior to all this," said Jason. "Isn't that still a possibility for how he became ill?"

"Yes, depending on what they were. And that could explain why only Cameron was affected. Maybe it was truly a coincidence that his medications chose that moment to interact, and there was never any poisoning going on."

"I suppose we're still waiting for Chief Conway to track down the details about the medications," said Jason. "Hopefully he's called Cameron's pharmacy by now, assuming Aaron gave him the contact information."

"Cameron said the pills were in his ditty bag, but Aaron couldn't find them, or so he said. Cameron said he was taking something for a cold as well."

Anita jumped in. "I remember from that Wikipedia article that some cold medicines can cause an interaction with some antidepressants that produce a belladonna-like reaction."

"True," said Christie, "but Cameron said he's on a medicine for anxiety, not depression."

"I know for a fact that there are medications that can be used for both conditions," said Anita. "I had to do some reading about that because of some of the kids at school who take them. So it could still be one of the culprits."

"That's encouraging," said Christie. "I think." She managed a grim smile.

"I'm not sure I understand why Conway doesn't ask Michelle directly what was in that package," said Anita. "Especially if there's the possibility that it could relate to Cameron's collapse."

Jason answered. "Let's assume he will be following up on that now that he's been made aware of its existence. There may be a simple answer."

The dinners arrived. The combination of aromas from chicken parmesan, shrimp scampi, chicken broccoli Alfredo and grilled salmon smelled delicious. A basket of warm, toasted garlic French bread accompanied the main courses. Nathan refilled the wine glasses.

"Yum," said Christie after a bite of her shrimp scampi. "This is delectable."

Nathan teased, "That's a big word for a small-town girl."

"You forget that I lived in San Francisco for ten years before moving back to White Castle," Christie retorted. "They use big words like that there."

"But you worked for a furniture company," said Anita. "I'm trying to imagine using the word 'delectable' to describe a sofa."

"How about a 'delectable divan'?" Jason laughed at his own attempt at a sales pitch.

"Speaking of divans, that reminds me of diving and of Hailey's snorkeling incident," said Christie. "Do you know anything new, Nathan?"

"Glad you asked." He wiped his lips and set his fork down on the plate. "I got an update from Uncle Conan earlier today. Hailey's going to be okay and is being released from the hospital tomorrow. She has to wait three days before she can fly, but they'll be home Wednesday."

"I'm sure her mom and dad are happy to know she's all right after all," said Christie.

"She'll fully recover from her injury," said Nathan, "but I don't know how she's going to take the news about her parents getting divorced."

"Oh, that's right," said Christie. "I already forgot about that."

"That's not good news," said Christie, her cell phone to her ear. "But thanks for letting me know." She groaned and rolled her head back as she ended the call.

"What's not good news?" she heard Aunt Doris ask from the flower room. "Who called you?"

"Why me?" Christie stomped around for a moment, gritting her teeth. She breathed deeply and said, "That was Conway. He's been the major bearer of bad news the past week. I'm not liking Mondays lately."

"Are you going to tell me what he said?" asked her aunt. "Is it about that young man from the wedding reception?"

Christie heaved again. "Yes. Cameron's taken a turn for the worse. It's been ten days since the big collapse, and he should be well or dead by now if it was really some kind of poisoning. At least that's what I think I read about in this kind of situation." She picked up an order from the stack and started selecting blooms for the tall vase she had selected.

"What else did Conway say, Honey?"

"The doctors are running more tests. They're puzzled, too, he said. Cameron had been getting better until last evening. There was even some talk about being discharged soon, but that's not on the table now. At least not for today."

"I'm so sorry to hear that," Aunt Doris commiserated. "Did Conway say anything about his partner, Aaron? How is he taking this turn of events?"

"Well, of course, my name is mud again. He's ready to blame me even though I'm the one who helped him out at the reception." Christie snorted and placed several stems of rose-pink carnations in the tall, gold-colored vase with burgundy bottle-brush flowers. She stepped back to assess the look, smiled, and added more of each, followed by white baby's breath to add some contrast.

Doris looked up from the tabletop arrangement she was working on. "I like how you've used the softer-petaled carnations to play off those sharp-ended bottlebrush flowers. It's going to be lovely when you're done."

Christie smiled. "Thank you. I learned a lot of this from you." She blew her aunt a kiss, then dropped her shoulders and stood at the side of the table, a few silvery-green eucalyptus stems in her hand. "You know, if Cameron dies, Aaron's probably going to go after me, and I'll lose my shop and everything." Tears welled up in her eyes.

Doris stepped around the worktable and put her hands on Christie's shoulders. "We both know you didn't do anything. You just wait and see; things will work out." She hugged her niece and let her sob for a moment.

Christie grabbed a tissue. "Thanks, Auntie. I know you're right, but it doesn't help right now, especially after that newspaper article. I have to figure out what really happened. I must be missing some important detail that would make sense of all this."

"What about Anita's friend, Nathan? Wasn't he working on something that you thought might be connected to all this?"

"Maybe. It seems to me that the timing of the threats to the Omega plant is related to the wedding. Does someone have a personal vendetta against Conan Starr? Did that someone—assuming he or she is acting alone—know that other family members would be here? I'm talking about Aaron, of course. I can't think of a way that anyone would have known Nathan Starr would be called in to the Omega plant and would be here also." Christie sighed. "I just can't figure it out."

"Do you think Nathan is any closer to tracing the origin of the threats?" Aunt Doris finished making a dark blue bow for the arrangement in front of her and tucked it into the low-profile bowl.

"I don't know. I haven't heard any more from Nathan since the four of us—Jason and I and Nathan and Anita—had dinner Saturday night."

Doris chuckled. "You seem to be seeing a lot of that Jason lately, even if you say you're not dating." She arched a brow.

Christie felt her face redden. "I'm not sure what to call it. I guess we're dating, but I refuse to say we're going steady. That's so high school!" She laughed, and Doris joined her.

Christie glanced at the front door when she noticed movement in front of the window. "Uh, oh. It's Conway." She wiped her hands on the towel lying on the table and met him halfway across the room.

"Are you here to arrest me, Chief?"

Conway furrowed his brow. "Should I?"

"No, sir. I'm just wondering why you're here. You already told me Cameron is worse over the phone."

"I have some other news that hit my desk a few minutes after I called you. I thought I should tell you in person."

"Okay. Is it good news or bad news?"

Conway reached into his pocket and pulled out his ever-present notebook. He put on his reading glasses and shuffled through the pages until he found what he wanted. "I was able to get the name of that medicine that Cameron is taking for his condition. It's called p-h-e-n-e-l-p-e-r-i-z-i-n-e. The brand name is Gadoifene." He looked at Christie. "I've never heard of it."

"Same here," said Christie. "Did you talk to the doctors at the hospital about it? I'm sure they can tell you more about its use and interactions."

"I just got this email from the pharmacy, and I'm on my way there now."

"Do you mind if I check it out while you're here?" Christie asked as she pulled her cell phone from her back pocket.

Conway held the paper for Christie to read. She quickly entered the name of the medication into the phone's search engine. Her eyes widened as she read through the long list of side effects and potential drug interactions. "I certainly wouldn't want to ever have to take this medicine," she said to Conway. "It can kill you." She showed him the screen.

She and Conway looked at each other, eyes wide.

CHAPTER 33

hile disappointed that Conway didn't invite her to go to the hospital, Christie had to admit that there wasn't any real good reason for him to do so. She looked at the list of orders for flowers for a funeral that was to take place on Thursday, grateful for the business after the unfortunate newspaper story in the Friday edition of the *White Castle Gazette*. Even if it was mostly for funerals. But then again, there were a lot more funerals in her hometown than weddings. She felt a sense of sadness rising through her chest.

"Well, Auntie, at least our customers aren't worried about ordering our 'killer flowers' for their loved ones who are already dead." She looked at her aunt with a half-grin but quickly changed her expression and said soberly, "That wasn't funny, was it?"

Aunt Doris clucked her tongue. "You just have to give them a little time for the dust to settle. Everything will be fine. Your grandma went through tough times and always came out okay. Now, come back here and help me with this order for the PTA meeting tonight."

The president of the White Castle Elementary School PTA

was a dear friend of her mother's, which probably explained the order for twenty tabletop arrangements for their annual Mother-Daughter Tea. It was an old-fashioned tradition that Christie remembered from her own grade school days. Each child made something in art class for his or her mother. The first-graders' gifts were the most primitive, such as alphabet pasta messages pasted onto scrolls made from popsicle sticks. By the time the students reached fifth grade, the artwork was more advanced. Christie wondered if her mother still had the pressed copper image of a squirrel that she had proudly created as a fifth-grader. She chuckled at the memory.

A Bach concerto for flute and orchestra played softly in the background as Christie and her aunt worked together.

"Did you say that Mrs. Anderson is going to pick these up instead of having them delivered?" Christie asked while placing yet another floral arrangement in the cooler. She counted the finished bouquets. "Four more to go, and we're done."

"Yes, honey. She has an SUV and asked that we put them in those low-sided cardboard trays for transport. She said she'll bring a couple of teenagers to help. I think she has twin boys, sophomores maybe by now."

Christie giggled. "I wonder if she bribed them with a promise to let them practice driving. They should be sixteen or close to it if they're sophomores, being as it's the end of the school year."

The shop's phone rang. Christie was closer to it, so she picked it up. Most of the time, Aunt Doris answered the calls because she liked to take the orders and let Christie handle the front of the shop.

"Christie's Flower Shoppe. How can I help you?" She picked up a pen out of habit, ready to write down details. "Yes, I can have those ready for you by four today. What kind of an arrangement would you like?" Christie scribbled her notes, nodding as she listened to the caller. "Thank you for calling. We'll see you later today."

Christie furrowed her brow as she put the phone down.

"Who was it?" asked Aunt Doris. "You have a funny look on your face."

"That was Mrs. Fremmerlid, my high school English teacher. She wants a bouquet to take to the newspaper office."

"What? Why would she do that?"

"She said she wants to support me and send them a message at the same time," said Christie.

"What's the message?"

"She wants me to write 'Support your local businesses' on the card. Isn't that sweet?"

"I hope they don't throw them back at her," replied her aunt as she finished making a bow for the vase sitting on the table in front of her.

The phone rang again. "Christie's Flower Shoppe. How can I help you?" Christie turned toward her aunt and mouthed, "Another order" while writing down the details.

"That was Emma Kangas from the print shop. She ordered a bouquet that she is taking to the newspaper office as well."

"Did she ask for the same message?" Aunt Doris placed the eighteenth arrangement in the cooler.

"Exactly. She told me that each of the women in the White Castle Women's Club will be ordering flowers and delivering them to the newspaper office. Most of the women are small-business owners, and some are already retired from their careers. I'm guessing they understand the impact of irresponsible reporting and what it can do to our types of businesses. They plan to order three or four arrangements every day this week." Christie felt tears welling up. "That's amazing. You know, showing their support for me. And sending a message to the newspaper at the same time."

Christie fielded two more calls for floral bouquets over the next half hour. When she finished the calls, she said to her aunt,

"Let's make each of them as different as we can so Jill, the *Gazette's* editor, can see the range of what we do."

"That's a great idea, young lady. And that's good advertising on your part. Let's finish these table decorations for the PTA, and we can get started on them. It almost feels like we're helping with some kind of protest, but I love the fact that our fellow small-business owners are reaching out to you."

"I don't know how much foot traffic the paper gets in their office," said Christie, "but anyone who drops in would see these as well, and it might trigger a little more business." Christie's chest swelled with pride and a sense of relief. Then she had a second thought. "That is if they display them at all."

Christie sent her aunt home for lunch after they finished the latest round of bouquets. Conway called to report that he had talked with Cameron's doctor and that the physician would order laboratory studies to see if that medication had been in his bloodstream. Her mind wandered back to her musings about the missing link between Cameron and the threats at Omega and the wedding reception. Were they all connected? Or not? She remembered that she'd planned to ask Nathan about the phone call that had been made directly to Conan Starr at work.

"Sorry to bother you at work, Nathan," Christie said, then explained her reason for calling.

"What do you need to know?"

"It sure seems odd that the newest threats at Omega seemed to coincide with Hailey's wedding."

"Why would that make a difference?" Nathan replied. "Young people get married all the time."

"True, but think about it this way: Conan's daughter is getting married in his hometown and it's the biggest wedding around here. It's a momentous occasion for the family. What if someone was trying to take advantage of his possible distraction to engineer a serious threat?"

Nathan said, "Hmm. That only makes sense if the threats

were coming from someone who has some knowledge of Conan's personal life."

"This is a small community, Nathan. I'll bet half of the employees at Omega live within thirty miles and that would include White Castle. And some of them may have even been invited to the wedding because he probably socializes with some of the upper-level employees. Michelle strikes me as someone who loves to rub shoulders with important people."

"I still don't see that as a viable likelihood. Why would any of his coworkers, especially if they are also his social peers, do such a thing?"

"I'm not saying they would be involved," said Christie, "but they'd know about the wedding and talk about it to others. Or what if it's not someone who works at Omega, but is a former employee who got fired? Or someone that Aaron knows from his activist group who also knows about the wedding?"

"I'm not following your logic, Christie. I don't think there even *is* any logic."

Christie exhaled loudly. "I don't know what it means either, but I think there's some connection. I don't believe Cameron was the intended victim if there really was poisoning involved. So, who was? Aaron said one of those three drinks was for you. Maybe you were the target. I mean, there are threats against Omega, you're the person doing the investigating, and you attended the wedding. A perfect trifecta!"

Nathan said, "Well, if someone was unhappy enough about Omega to send them threats, you'd think they'd be pleased I'm investigating them, right? Besides, no one knows for sure if one of those drinks was poisoned, Christie. And to answer your question about that telephone call, we're still working on it. I do know it was a cell phone, but that's all I can tell you for sure."

"Okay," said Christie. "Thanks for hearing me out anyway."

"I understand that you're trying to help. And so am I. Goodbye, Christie. I need to get back to my work."

Christie collapsed into the chair at her desk. Stormy jumped down from her perch and hopped into her owner's lap. She purred her sympathy as Christie idly ran her fingers through the cat's silky black fur.

"What am I going to do, Stormy? What am I missing? No, make that what is *Chief Conway* missing?"

CHAPTER 34

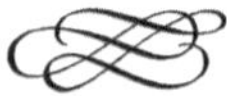

*L*ate in the afternoon, Christie looked up from her desk when the front door chimed the arrival of a customer. She squealed when she saw her friend Missy waltz in from the street. She jumped up, disrupting Stormy's siesta, and ran to meet her with a hug.

"Missy! How wonderful to see you! Are you here to work on your wedding plans?"

Missy grinned and replied, "Since it's only five months until September, I thought we should get started. Is this a good time?"

"It's perfect. But why aren't you at work today?"

"I had some business in Chehalis, and when I was done with the meeting, I realized I was only thirty minutes away from White Castle and decided to drop in. I hoped I wouldn't need an appointment because it was a spur-of-the-moment decision on my part."

Christie smiled and shook her head. "Monday afternoons are typically quiet, and Aunt Doris will handle the walk-in business if I ask." She led the way to her consultation corner in the back of the shop. "Aunt Doris?"

"Yes, I'll keep an eye out for customers while you meet with

Missy. And I'll take care of those flowers that are going to be picked up in a little while."

Missy walked back to the flower room to give Doris a hug. "It's so nice to see you again, Aunt Doris. It feels like forever since last fall when that old desk brought you and Christie into my life."

Doris's cheeks turned pink. "Christie told me you and Brian are getting married here in White Castle. And that she's going to do your wedding flowers. That'll be nice."

Missy giggled in her soft voice. "I couldn't imagine anyone else doing the flowers. I know they'll be lovely."

Once Missy and Christie were settled at the desk in the back, Christie said, "I have to tell you that there's a possibility I won't be in business anymore in September."

Missy covered her mouth with her hand. "No! Why not? I thought you loved doing this."

"It's not because I don't love my business, but one of the guests nearly died at a wedding recently where I had done the floral arrangements. Unfortunately, one of the flowers I used had the name of belladonna in it, although it was not in the deadly nightshade family. But just the word belladonna makes people think of poison thanks to those old mystery stories. Anyway, the local newspaper published an unflattering account and is labeling my bouquets as 'killer flowers' again." Christie scoffed.

"Which is exactly why you wouldn't do anything like that," said Missy. "That would be so obvious."

"Yeah, I know." Christie sighed. "If I can just get through one full year of business, and that will be in October, I think I'll be okay. But there's a whole summer ahead of me right now, and Chief Conway hasn't solved his case yet, and the newspaper article just came out." Christie briefly told her about the wedding, the reception and the threats to the father of the bride because of the nuclear plant.

"Can I do anything to help? Can Brian?" Missy asked as she thumbed through a bridal magazine.

"I don't think so unless you know how to trace telephone calls to nuclear plants."

"Well, Brian's an electrician, but it's not very likely that he knows how to do that. He would if he could, I'm sure. But my daughter Lynette's fiancé is in telecommunications. I wonder if Sean could help."

"Really? I can talk to Nathan Starr about working with Sean. He works for the Nuclear Regulatory Commission and has been trying to determine who is responsible for recent threats and calls to Omega."

"Then I'll talk to Lynette and Sean. Now, let's talk about flowers. You realize, Christie, that even if you don't have an official shop, you can still do wedding flowers as a private enterprise."

CHRISTIE HUMMED a few lines of "The Wedding March" as she spiffed up the shop at the end of the day. She was feeling more optimistic about the possibility of finding the mysterious nuclear threat caller after chatting with Missy. And she felt confident that the blood tests on Cameron would establish that he was indeed taking the medicine that could have caused his collapse in the first place. Life was looking up. Her phone buzzed in her pocket. Conway's name was on the screen. Her heart dropped.

"This is Christie."

"Conway here. Dr. Pence just called me. There wasn't enough blood from the initial draws to run that drug-level test on Cameron."

"Oh, rats." Christie felt like the air was knocked out of her lungs. "Did he say anything about drawing fresh blood samples to see if it was still in his blood?"

"Actually, I asked about doing that. He wasn't keen on the idea because it's now been about ten days since the wedding, but I told him that if there was even a trace of the medication still in his bloodstream, it could help establish the medicine as being at least part of the problem."

"And did he say he'd do it?"

"Yes, he did."

"That's good, but, as you said, it's been a long time since he would have taken his last dose, and the new tests may not show anything."

"We can only wait and see."

"True." Christie sighed. "Hey. That reminds me of something else. Did you ever get all the test results from the flowers that you took from my shop? Were they able to prove that there was any of the bad kind of belladonna in them?"

Conway groaned into her ear. "Thanks for the reminder. I haven't heard from them at all. I'll call the evidence lab and see what the final assessment was. And I'll get back to you."

"Thanks."

Aunt Doris had been listening in on Christie's half of the conversation as usual, which was easy in the small shop. "Was that Conway again? What did he say this time?"

"Another false hope dashed! He said there wasn't enough blood left in the lab from Cameron's first drug test."

"What was his answer to drawing more blood now?"

"The doctor said he would, but it may be too late to prove it was ever in his bloodstream."

"You just hang in there, Christie. The truth will come out eventually. It always does."

Christie busied herself with the wedding plan template she'd filled out when Missy was in the shop. She smiled despite the gloom she was feeling when she reviewed the colors and flower styles that they'd discussed. Missy wanted a romantic setting of soft blues and lavenders set off with dashes of yellow and white.

Christie drew a few sketches of what she thought Missy had in mind. She'd talk to Anita as well because she had a real flair for dramatic creations. It occurred to Christie that maybe she and Anita could create some kind of sideline of wedding planning down the road. Once she got past the 'Cameron affair,' as she thought of it.

She flipped through her wedding planning book for the pictures she'd tucked away. She wanted to create the magical atmosphere that Missy deserved after waiting so many years for her marriage to Brian. She came across the picture from Hailey's wedding and sighed. What was it about that glass that bothered her? She opened the desk drawer and pulled out a magnifying glass to study the berries. They looked like ordinary blueberries, even when magnified.

Her cell phone rang, breaking the spell. Anita's name was on the screen. "Hi, Anita. How was the school zoo today?"

"Hey. Don't get me started. I can hardly wait for this school year to end. And it's only April."

Christie laughed, recalling her own eagerness to be outside playing ball or shooting hoops instead of being trapped indoors on a sunny spring day. "What's up?"

"I was just calling to see if you wanted to get together for dinner and another mystery-solving episode. You can ask Jason if he's available, and I'll bring Nathan."

"Sure. Where and when?"

"Silver Spoon Saloon at six."

"Great. I'll see you there. I'll call Jason." She tucked the photo and magnifying glass in her purse. Anita knew more than she did about plants and berries.

CHAPTER 35

$\mathcal{I}$t was a quiet night at the bar on a Monday—at least it would be quiet until the trivia game started at seven thirty. It seemed that all of the local bars were hosting trivia nights, with groups of people showing up trying to win the most points. All for a small gift card good for more beer.

After being served their beers and ordering hamburger specials, Anita began. "Nathan and I were talking about the wedding reception and Cameron's collapse, of course." She glanced at Nathan, who nodded subtly. "We think Christie might be onto something. She wondered if Nathan was the real target, considering that Aaron offered him one of those drinks, poisoned or not."

"But he was a last-minute guest, wasn't he?" queried Jason. "It seems like it would take some planning to set up the belladonna and all."

"I know for a fact that anyone can order belladonna in various forms, including seeds or liquid, and have them delivered within a couple of days," said Christie. "But how could the perpetrator have known that Nathan would be called in to investigate the threats? That would have to be someone on the inside, I would think."

"Anything to do with the nuclear plant would take your flowers out of the mystery," said Anita.

"I'm still puzzled that the wholesaler slipped in those belladonna lilies," said Christie.

"Did you ever call them to ask why they were added to your order?" asked Jason.

Christie shook her head, her golden curls bobbing with the movement.

"Can Christie sue the wholesaler for all the extra stress those lilies have caused?" asked Anita, only half-kidding.

"Thanks for the idea, Anita," said Christie, "but there still isn't any way that Cameron could have realistically ingested or eaten any of the flowers. They were pretty, but not tasty, I'm sure, plus they might have caused digestive issues, not central nervous system shutdown." She turned to Nathan. "Back to motives, there might be an issue that relates homophobia and the nuclear plant threats. Do you have any thoughts about the internal relationship issues in your family that might help identify the would-be murderer in either of those ways?"

He sat with his elbow on the table, chin resting on his hand. "Well, you already know how my dad and Uncle Doyle feel about gays, and neither one is particularly close to Uncle Conan, who is the most tolerant."

"What about Michelle? What does she say?" asked Jason.

"She hasn't said much, but according to Hailey, she was upset when she found out that Aaron was asked to be a groomsman." Nathan raised an eyebrow. "Michelle tried to talk Hailey and Ryan out of including him, but they were adamant. Besides, they'd already asked him and weren't about to rescind the invitation."

Anita added, "That would look bad, to say the least. But why weren't you included as a possible groomsman in the original plan? Or were you? Or are there family issues with you as well?"

Nathan grinned. "I've always been one of Michelle's favorites, or so I'm told, even though my dad and Uncle Conan weren't close. Hailey reached out to me early on, but with my unpredictable schedule that could have me anywhere in the country at any one point in time, I couldn't count on being readily available."

"Why was Doyle not invited to the wedding?" asked Christie.

"Uncle Doyle and Uncle Conan have had issues for as long as I can remember, although I never knew why. It wasn't something that grown-ups shared with kids. Even at Christmas time, Doyle and his family were excluded from our get-togethers. I just accepted it."

"Could Doyle have been jealous of Conan's success at his work or perhaps of the fancy wedding? Jealousy is always one of the possibilities in murder stories," said Anita. "I should know. I read enough of them. And I don't mean my students' essays, although what their message is can be a mystery in itself." The others laughed with her.

"From what I was told," said Christie, "Doyle and Conan both dated Michelle in high school. She dated Doyle first—they were in the same class, two years younger than Conan. Somewhere along the way, she switched to Conan, he being the football captain and she one of the cheerleaders. And Doyle ended up with one of her cousins instead."

"Yep. It's jealousy," said Anita with a nod and a smug grin on her face.

Nathan got back on the subject, saying, "I can't imagine that Uncle Doyle would stoop so low as to threaten the nuclear plant. Certainly not over the lack of an invitation to a wedding or still being upset about a high school romantic triangle that's more than two decades old."

"Does your dad get along with Doyle? Or Conan?" asked Christie.

Nathan winced. "Well, like I said, my father *is* homophobic and makes no secret of it, so he and Doyle aren't exactly close. He gets along with Conan for the most part, but none of the brothers are particularly warm and loving to each other."

"Sounds like the kind of family that only gets together for weddings and funerals, and only out of a sense of obligation," concluded Jason. "And just in time, here comes our server with our hamburgers."

They ate the juicy burgers, crisp french fries and onion rings with gusto, interrupted only when Christie's cell phone rang. She grimaced when she saw that it was Conway again.

"This is Christie. What's new, Chief?"

"Thought you'd want to know that the hospital lab found blood from one of Cameron's earlier days in the hospital that they could use to measure that medication level—phenyl-*something*-zine. But it'll take a couple of days for results because it has to go to a Seattle lab for testing."

"That's good to know. Maybe you're getting somewhere." Christie suppressed the urge to say something more unkind, opting to stay on his good side. "What about the evidence lab? Anything new there?"

"As you might expect, those tests also had to be sent out of town to the state's central lab in Olympia. There's a backlog, but I asked them to push our specimens to the head of the line. Dr. Pence made a special call to the head of the unit there, which might have helped. Turns out they were frat brothers in college."

"So those results are still in limbo for now?"

"Afraid so. Well, that's all I have. Good night."

"Thanks." Christie briefed the others. "If the tests show that Cameron did have that medicine on board, that could explain everything." She managed a thin smile.

Anita added, "And then Conway could give the newspaper an update, and they can retract that 'killer flowers' headline."

Christie raised an index finger. "Oh, that reminds me of something. Missy came into the shop today to talk about the flowers for her wedding."

"Who's Missy?" asked Nathan.

"She's a special person who we helped last fall. I'll fill you in later," said Anita. "Go on, Christie."

"Anyway, I told her about the situation with the shop, and when I told her about the threats at Omega and the strange phone calls, she said her daughter's fiancé works in some kind of high-level telecommunications. Maybe he could help you, Nathan, with the origin of that last call to Conan's personal office phone."

"Hmm. I'm not getting very far with my own staff. I could certainly check with my boss and see if she's okay with going outside our normal channels."

"Hey, it couldn't hurt," said Jason. "And it could help a lot. I know the nuclear plant isn't Conway's responsibility, but as Christie said, maybe the threats are related to whoever hurt Cameron. And knowing who made the call could help Conway solve that crime."

"I can call Missy and get the contact information for you," said Christie. "I really want to be able to stay in business for her wedding. Oh. I brought something." She reached into her tote and pulled out the photo enlargement and her magnifying glass. "I almost forgot this."

Nathan whistled. "Just like Sherlock Holmes."

Christie wrinkled her nose at him and placed the print on the table in front of Anita and Nathan. "Check out the glass. Nathan, could it be the same one that you got from Aaron?"

Nathan reached over to take the magnifying lens from Anita and studied the glass, then looked at the people who were standing in the background. "I'll be damned. What is Aaron doing back there?"

184

CHAPTER 36

The four of them took turns studying the photo. Aaron was standing in front of another table to the right of the bar, where the punch bowls were sitting on the counter. His back was to the camera, but he appeared to be doing something with his right hand while looking toward the left. To his right, about five feet away, was his dad, his back also to the camera. Standing across the table from Doyle was Michelle with a scowl on her face.

"He looks guilty to me," said Anita.

"But guilty of what?" asked Nathan.

"It looks like he's checking to see if anyone is watching him," said Christie. "And his dad may be doing the same thing."

"Watching him do what?" asked Jason.

"I don't know," Christie wailed. "Do you think we should ask him?"

"Ask him what, exactly?" asked Anita. "For all we know, he could have been turning his head because someone called his name, and he was looking to see who it was."

Jason said, "I agree with you, Anita. I don't think we can make this into anything more than that."

Christie took the magnifying glass from Jason once more and studied the image. She took a big swallow of her wine then sat back in her chair, one leg crossed over the other, arms across her chest. "Okay, gang. Michelle and Doyle appear to be talking about something. I don't suppose they'll tell us what it was all about."

"It could have been something as simple as 'Congratulations on a great wedding, Michelle,'" said Jason. "Not everything has to be part of a mystery."

"Michelle's face doesn't look like Doyle said something nice like that, although you could be right," said Christie. She frowned while she pondered her next move. "Back to Cameron's possible reaction—what if I call Aaron and ask him about that cough medicine now that I know what prescription he was taking? Do you think that would be a reasonable question to ask?"

"I think that would be okay," said Jason. "It shows interest in Cameron without throwing any blame around."

Nathan and Anita nodded.

"Okay," said Christie, phone in hand. "I'll call."

Aaron answered on the second ring.

"Hey. This is Christie. I was wondering how Cameron is doing after his last episode. Do you have an update?"

"Actually, I'm at the hospital and was just going back in to see Cameron now. He's awake again."

"Before you hang up, did you ever figure out what cough medicine he was taking? I presume you know Conway got the name of his other medicine from Cameron's pharmacy. He asked Dr. Pence about it at the hospital, and it sounds like it's complicated to use, or at least challenging with certain foods and other drugs."

"It was one of those over-the-counter cough and cold medicines that covers all the symptoms—you know, like cough and runny nose. I remember it had a DM on the end of it. The pharmacist said that means it had dextromethorphan in it for his cough."

"I've used that myself. Do you know if the pharmacist warned Cameron about any drug interactions?"

"I wasn't with him at the time, but Cameron is usually quite cautious and actually reads the fine print even though most people don't."

"What about some of the foods that interact with Cameron's anxiety medicine? Do you know if he avoids them? Some of them were common things like cheddar cheese."

"Yeah. In general, I know he does, but sometimes he forgets, or maybe he takes a small bite of something he shouldn't eat because he wants to taste it. And it's hard to remember all of the foods—it's a long list. I try to watch him, but we're not together twenty-four/seven."

"What about alcohol? If I remember correctly, it's also on the list of things to avoid."

"He usually doesn't drink at all because his doctor was very clear about how bad the reaction could be. He's discovered he can drink a small amount of alcohol without a reaction, but he only does that when we're celebrating something special. Some of our friends tease him that he must be a 'friend of Bill' because of it." Aaron chuckled. "I'm not sure Cameron even knows what they mean; he's pretty naïve. I find myself protecting him a lot."

"He sounds like a sweet young man," said Christie. "One more question. Did you know your dad was going to be at the wedding and reception?"

"Not at all. He said he was going to stay away, so I was very surprised to see him in the back pew and again at the reception. I was expecting fireworks at first, but he seemed to be getting along with the family okay, at least until Uncle Arthur said some things. It would have been nice if Dad had stood up a bit more for me to Uncle Arthur, but, well, I shouldn't have expected that anyway. I was already disappointed that Dad didn't come over to visit with Cameron and me right away when we all got to the reception, but that's just how he is. Like I've mentioned before."

"Well, I won't keep you any longer so you can visit Cameron. Please tell him 'Hi' from me. And thank you for your help."

Nathan had ordered a second round of drinks and a plate of nachos while Christie was on the phone. She helped herself to a handful of the cheesy tortilla chips and drank a couple of swallows of beer while processing what she'd learned from Aaron.

"Are you going to share the rest of the conversation?" asked Anita, impatient to know more. "You know, the part we couldn't hear."

Christie set her beer down. "Oh, yeah. Well, Aaron confirmed that Cameron was taking a cold medication with dextromethorphan in it, and I know that's on the list of contraindications for his medicine. He also avoids alcohol, which is on that list, too, but there was a glass on the floor where we found Cameron. I didn't sniff it, but what if it had alcohol and he drank it? Could that be the culprit?"

"It would sure be nice if Cameron were able to tell us the rest of the story," said Jason. "It seems that everything hangs on him. Maybe his collapse was a simple case of food or alcohol interfering with his phenylperizine."

Christie nodded. "His reaction may be related to that cold medicine, alcohol, even cheese or some combination of all the above, but there's still a possibility that Cameron may not have been taking his anxiety medicine at the time of his collapse. If it doesn't show up in the blood tests, it doesn't matter whether or not he took cold medicine, ate cheese or had a drink."

They were quiet for a moment as they sipped their beers and pondered the possibilities.

"Seeing Uncle Doyle at the reception bothers me," said

Nathan. "He supposedly said he wasn't attending, but we saw him at the church, and then he showed up at the reception. Why?"

"And Aaron talks as though he and his dad don't get along at all, and there they are standing just a few feet from each other in the picture," said Christie. "I don't get it."

CHAPTER 37

*C*hristie slept fitfully. She couldn't shake the image of Aaron and Doyle together and still didn't have an adequate explanation for the empty cocktail glass on the floor next to Cameron.

When her alarm went off at six thirty Tuesday morning, she dragged herself out of bed and turned on her coffeemaker, adding an extra measure of grounds to make it stronger than usual. Stormy had merely opened an eye and stayed in bed. Christie idly wondered if caffeine worked on cats as it did on humans. Three cups of coffee later, she was showered and dressed and was ready to face the day.

AUNT DORIS WAS ALREADY busy making half a dozen bouquets for a funeral taking place later that day. Stormy hopped up to her observation post. She turned three circles before settling in place, her eyes toward the front door. Christie joined her aunt at the worktable in the flower room. Doris handed her the small pile of orders that had been lying at the end of the table. Christie perused the orders and saw that three of them were for tabletop gardens, which could be enjoyed for much longer than the more typical floral arrangements. She selected a medium-sized vase and began choosing stems of flowers and foliage.

Doris looked up from her work. "You're smiling today, Christie. Do you have some kind of good news for a change?"

"Yes, Auntie. At least, I think so. Guess who was in that picture from the wedding, the one with the cocktail glass on the table?"

"You know I wouldn't have any idea because I didn't go to the reception, so you'll just have to tell me."

"Oh, that's right. Anyway, Nathan looked at the photo last night when we were at the Silver Spoon and he noticed his Uncle Doyle, Aaron's dad, in the background standing near Aaron."

"So? Why would that be a surprise?"

"Aaron and his dad aren't particularly close, and they'd had words not long before that picture was taken. Earlier, Aaron told me his dad wasn't going to be at the wedding or reception. Supposedly, he hadn't been invited."

"Do you think Aaron was lying about his dad?"

"No. I called him last evening, and he swore he didn't know his dad was going to be there. I didn't tell him about the picture, but it seemed odd that he would be anywhere near Doyle except by accident."

"Hm. It sounds like Aaron might be afraid of his dad."

Christie scowled. "I don't think it's fear. He may not want to say anything that might jeopardize their relationship. Aaron said he's been working on it, so Doyle would be more accepting of Cameron. I'd guess it's still rocky, but at least they were in the same building."

"That sounds promising. Have you heard any more about Aaron's friend? Last I heard, he'd had a relapse."

"Aaron mentioned that Cameron was a little better and was

awake again. He was on his way to see him when I called. That's all I know about that."

Christie stepped back to admire the cluster of blue, coral, and white flowers with two types of foliage in a cobalt blue vase. Satisfied, she set it in the cooler for delivery later.

She continued. "I decided I should show the photo with Aaron and Doyle in it to Conway. They're standing next to the punch bowls. Maybe Doyle poisoned Cameron's punch somehow when Aaron was about to deliver it."

"But wasn't that photo taken after Aaron had already taken the three drinks Michelle offered earlier to their respective tables?"

"Hm. Yes, I guess so, considering I see a drink on the table in the foreground. But what if Cameron asked for a second glass, and Doyle fixed it for him? He could have added the poison then and given it to Aaron to give to Cameron."

Doris nodded, her lips curled. "Plausible, but doesn't seem likely. Are you suggesting that Doyle just happened to be at the punch bowl table when Cameron just happened to ask for a second drink?"

Christie shrugged. "Anyway, I called earlier, and Conway said he'd come by and take a look."

Aunt Doris raised an eyebrow above the tortoiseshell-framed, half-moon reading glasses that she wore for working with flowers and said, "The chief's like a dog with a bone, you know."

"And dogs can usually be distracted by a bigger bone." Christie winked at her aunt and selected another vase for the next arrangement.

As she had predicted, Conway showed up at the shop about fifteen minutes later.

"What's this news you say you have for me?" He leaned his tall frame against Christie's counter where she sat at her laptop creating invoices for the funeral flowers.

Christie produced the photo enlargement for him. She explained what she and her friends had noticed the evening before and proposed the theory that Doyle had poisoned Cameron after all.

"This picture doesn't prove anything except that Aaron, his dad and Michelle were standing near each other by the punch bowls. You're grasping at straws, Christie. That young Nathan Starr could have done exactly the same thing, you know."

"And his motive would be?"

"I'm working on that."

"But don't you want to know the truth of what happened to Cameron? And did you hear that he was awake again last night? Aaron was on his way to talk to him when I chatted with him last evening."

"Tell you what I'll do, Christie. I'll go to see Cameron and ask Aaron about what he was doing when this photo was taken." He folded it and put it with the notebook in his pocket. "The test results about that medication might be back by now also."

He turned on his heel and left.

CHAPTER 38

*M*issy called Christie mid-afternoon with contact information for her daughter's fiancé, Sean. "Lynette said he does something for the Department of Justice that has to do with cyber-tracking and that tracing calls like the one Nathan has for him is what he was trained to do. He's expecting to hear from your friend soon."

"That's wonderful, Missy. I'll share the info with Nathan as soon as I get off the phone. Maybe this will be the missing piece of information that will help Chief Conway nail the right person."

"Glad to help. I'll come down in a couple of weeks, and we can plan some more for my wedding. Lynette wants to go dress shopping with me. It's been so wonderful to be able to spend time with her, the daughter you helped me find."

Christie felt tears in her eyes as she recalled the events of the previous Halloween that led up to connecting Missy and Brian, as well as their love-child daughter, Lynette. "I hope you enjoy every one of those precious moments. You've earned them. See you soon."

She texted Nathan next, as promised, and then helped a

couple of women who were looking for birthday gifts. Christie congratulated herself on her success in selecting several lines of gift items that turned out to be popular with the local clientele. She found herself smiling every time she sat down to order inventory replacements.

While her first love would always be creating fabulous floral displays that made their recipients smile, she knew she wouldn't be able to survive in business without the ancillary sales of cards and trinkets. She'd learned that lesson from her Grandma Maude O'Mara who had started the flower shop after her own children were grown. Even though she had opened the store as more of a hobby, she'd had to prove to Grandpa O'Mara that she could make money at it. And she had, much to his initial surprise.

In the aftermath of the 'killer flowers' headline of the previous Friday, Christie was also grateful for the orders that came in every day for delivery to the newspaper office with the "support your local businesses" message.

The door alarm chimed and Christie looked up, noting that it was about time that the mail was typically delivered. Instead of the mail carrier that she anticipated, she saw Aaron and Chief Conway entering together. She got up and met them halfway to the door.

"Good afternoon, Chief. Hi, Aaron. I'm guessing that you've come from the hospital. How is Cameron?"

"He's much better, Christie," said Aaron. "Dr. Pence thinks he can be discharged tomorrow if all goes well."

"That's great news." Christie smiled. "Did Dr. Pence figure out why he had the relapse?"

Conway cleared his throat. "It appears that Cameron had a visitor a couple of hours before the relapse. We didn't know about it until today."

"How would that cause a relapse? And who would be visiting him here? Aaron said he doesn't have any close family." Christie looked from one face to the other.

"Cameron said it was a woman who told him she was a volunteer at the hospital," said Aaron. "She seemed to know who Cameron was but didn't identify herself. She brought him a bouquet of flowers and left a muffin for him."

Conway added, "The nurse said that the volunteers don't enter patient rooms without checking with the staff first, and they all wear official badges. She was quite sure there weren't any volunteers on the floor that morning. Apparently, Cameron started complaining about being dizzy after he ate half of the unauthorized muffin, and then his blood pressure dropped, and he went out again. Fortunately, his nurse was in his room at the time and called for help, and he was given the right medicine to reverse the problem."

"Do you have any idea who this woman was?" Christie felt her pulse going faster. Could this be the person who had poisoned Cameron earlier?

"Not yet," said Conway. "The hospital security manager is going to collect the tapes from Monday for the time period involved. We'll get a chance to look at them later."

"What about the muffin? Did anyone think to test it to see if it was the cause of the problem?"

"A quick-thinking nurse put it aside and showed it to the doctor after the crisis was resolved. It was sent to the toxicology lab when the nurse told the doctor about it." He pulled out a notepad and read his notes. "It's now Wednesday and that happened on Monday, so the report could be out later today. Dr. Pence said it usually takes about forty-eight hours turnaround time because it has to go to the central lab in Portland."

"Maybe this will be the breakthrough to solving the whole mystery," said Christie.

"I don't understand who would want to hurt Cameron," said Aaron. "I hope the security footage shows who it was."

Conway pocketed his notepad and pen. "If you want to look at the tapes with me, Aaron, I'm going to the hospital later today.

The security office will have them ready by about three if you're free."

Aaron perked up. "I'll meet you there, although I probably won't recognize the person, as I don't know anyone from around here except my own family."

Christie breathed a sigh of relief, and the men left. She wondered if she would recognize the woman who had visited him, but it was more important that Aaron see the security files. Having been back in town for a mere six months after being away from her hometown for ten years (fourteen, if she counted attending college out of town), she didn't know many of the local population herself, especially more recent newcomers. Aunt Doris, on the other hand, knew practically everybody, but asking her to go to the hospital to look at the security files was above the call of duty, at least for now.

The front door chimed again, and this time, it *was* the mail carrier. Christie smiled at the young woman who delivered the mail five days a week. "Hi, Lindsey," she said, accepting the small stack of envelopes, "I hope these aren't all bills today."

Lindsey grinned in reply. "You'd rather hear from Publisher's Clearing House, I suppose. Maybe you'll get lucky tomorrow," she said with a mini-salute.

Anita walked in as Lindsey exited. "Hey. Nathan just called. He said he talked to Sean and hoped to get some information from him by tomorrow. He also wanted to thank you for the contact information. Even his boss signed off on going outside the box for this special situation."

Christie related what she'd just learned from Aaron and Conway. "Maybe those files will give Conway the answer he needs. I only hope they have good cameras at the hospital and that they were working."

Anita nodded grimly with Christie.

CHAPTER 39

The seconds dragged by slowly for the rest of the
afternoon. Heather had picked up the orders to deliver
to the funeral home. Aunt Doris had created a couple of birthday
bouquets to be picked up by the end of the day. Three businesses
had called to order bouquets for the newspaper office. Christie
was catching up on her end-of-month bookkeeping entries.

She looked up to see who had set off the door chime and
jumped up to greet Hailey and Ryan. Hailey's left lower leg was
bandaged, and she limped slowly across the room with Ryan's
support but she had a huge smile on her face.

"I'm so happy to see you two," exclaimed Christie. "We've
all heard about your terrible accident." She glanced down at the
leg. "Are you going to be okay?"

Hailey smiled and said, "I'll be fine. The doctor in Puerto
Rico said I'd be good as new in a few weeks, except for a few
scars. The hardest part was having to repair a major artery where
the shark bit me after I cut my leg. He said Ryan did all the right
things and kept the blood loss down."

Ryan shrugged. "It's all that emergency training from my
Boy Scout days. I'm glad it came in handy."

"Me, too," said Christie. "So why are you here? You should be visiting your family."

"Mom picked us up at the airport, so she's already debriefed us," said Hailey. "She told us what happened to Cameron and how Chief Conway has been pestering you. Is there anything we can do to help?"

"Wow. That's sweet of you to offer," said Christie, "but hopefully, he'll have someone else to consider after he looks at the hospital's security footage today." In response to their puzzled looks, Christie told them about Cameron's story of a strange visitor.

"So Cameron's still in the hospital?" asked Hailey. "Is he going to be okay?"

"According to your cousin Aaron, he may be discharged tomorrow. He still has memory lapses, from what I understand, but he's alive, and that's the important part."

Hailey asked Ryan, "Do you mind if we go over to the hospital to see him? Aaron might be there as well."

Ryan put his arm around his new wife's shoulders and planted a small kiss on the top of her head, she being a good six inches shorter. "Whatever you want, Hailey."

Hailey hugged Christie. "I'm so sorry about this. I know my mom can be like the ice princess, but hopefully, Chief Conway can straighten everything out."

Christie's eyes followed the happy young couple as they exited. She guessed that Michelle hadn't mentioned her possible divorce yet. Christie gave her a silent nod to having at least a little bit of discretion.

Ten minutes later, while Christie continued reconciling the end-of-month accounts, a phone call from Jason temporarily rescued her from the depths of her spreadsheets.

"Sure, Jason. I'd love to meet you for dinner tonight. Where are we going?"

"There's a new Mexican restaurant in Ionia that one of my

clients raved about today. Can I pick you up at the house about six?"

"Do you mind if I call Anita and see if she wants to join us?"

"Sure. She and Nathan are both welcome if they want to meet us there."

Christie was spiffing up the shop, getting ready for the next day, when her cell phone vibrated in her pocket. She saw Conway's name, and though she normally dreaded his calls, she eagerly pressed the green icon to answer. "Christie here. I'm dying to know what you found out, Chief."

Conway exhaled loudly before saying anything. "Unfortunately, the hospital security cameras aren't placed in patient rooms, which is understandable, and they are few and far between in the hallways."

"Were you able to learn anything at all?"

"We saw the back of one woman who was otherwise unidentified walking down the hall toward Cameron's room, but the camera didn't record her entering the room, and we never saw a face. Aaron wasn't able to identify her at all."

"Oh, well. It was worth a try. What about the toxicology lab? Do you know anything about the muffin?"

"Now that's a different story," said Conway. "I'm told it looked like one of those lemon poppy seed muffins you can buy at the grocery store, and that's exactly what the lab reported on testing. Nothing poisonous about the muffin itself, so we went back and talked to Cameron some more about the woman who came to visit him. I thought maybe she had offered him something to drink as well, for lack of a better idea."

"And?"

"Turns out, the visitor brought him a bottle of orange juice, which Cameron drank while she waited. She took the empty bottle when she left. Said she'd put it in recycling for Cameron."

"Oh." Christie felt deflated again. "So if it did contain poison of some kind, there's no way to trace it now."

"I'm afraid not."

"There's got to be an explanation for his relapse and for that woman, Conway. By the way, did you ever talk to Doyle Starr about being at the reception when he supposedly hadn't been invited?"

"No. Why?"

"Well, you mentioned something to me a day or so back about how maybe Aaron and I were conspiring to hurt Cameron, which you and I both know is a ludicrous idea."

Conway was silent.

"I was thinking more about that picture from the reception that shows Doyle and Michelle across the table from each other. What if *they* were the ones conspiring?"

CHAPTER 40

After appeasing her spoiled cat with a homemade chicken dinner, Christie surveyed her closet. It wasn't quite warm enough yet to wear summer clothes, so she opted for a black jumper with a white long-sleeved tee and black tights and boots. A touch of blush and lipstick and she was ready to go out to try the new restaurant. She hoped they had good margaritas.

Las Pepitas was bursting at the seams with customers, which seemed surprising for a weeknight evening. Anita and Nathan had already scored a table in the back near the bar, where the noise level was slightly less than deafening.

"Is there a special occasion going on?" Christie asked once she was seated. She had to lean across the table to make herself heard.

"Not that I know of," said Anita. "But the word on this street is that the food is great, and the drinks are better."

Jason said, "I'll drink to that!" He would have accidentally hit the waitress who happened to arrive at that moment, but she swerved out of his way just in time.

"Drinks, you said?" she asked with a smile.

They all ordered margaritas on the rocks. Nathan added a

plate of loaded nachos as an appetizer. "I'm hungry. Didn't have time for lunch," he explained.

"Who wants to know what I learned today from Sean, Lynette's fiancé?" Nathan asked, a huge Cheshire Cat grin on his face. He wiggled his eyebrows for added effect.

Christie gave him a look. "We all do, of course. But me most of all, I think."

Nathan cleared his throat theatrically. "It turns out that he was able to trace the most recent calls to Omega from a phone that is registered to Conan Starr, Hailey's father."

"But that has to be wrong," Christie countered. "The calls were made *to* Conan Starr, not *from* him."

Nathan held up his hand. "Notice I said the phone was *registered* to Conan Starr, not that he was necessarily the user of said phone."

The waitress returned with a tray of drinks and the nachos, interrupting Christie's attempt to counter again. Before she could ask the next obvious question, Nathan held his glass in the air and said, "A toast to the experts in telecommunications!"

Christie tasted the margarita, which she pronounced excellent. "I presume there's a way to tell who was actually using the phone to make the call. Is there?"

"Not exactly, but by process of elimination using the GPS signals, we can exclude a couple of obvious people. It wasn't Conan, who was at the nuclear plant when the call was made from Arizona. It probably wasn't his daughter, Hailey, who was reportedly in California with her girlfriends for a bachelorette weekend, according to Facebook posts. It might have been his wife, Michelle, who would have had access but was presumably somewhere around White Castle at the time. This was the week before the wedding, as you may recall."

"Are you saying you still don't know for sure?" asked Christie.

"Correct," Nathan said, nodding. "It may have been a phone

that was used by someone close to him in the office to avoid some of that governmental red tape you may have heard about." He grinned. "Red tape is very real. I can vouch for that."

"So we're at a dead end here," said Christie. "Is that what you're saying? If you are, I'm canceling my toast to the telecommunications experts."

"Not so quick," said Nathan. "If this had been a company line or communication through its internal email system, I'd have more complete information. Unfortunately for us, this person went outside the system and it makes it harder to identify them. But not impossible."

"So there's hope?" Christie dared to ask.

"Sean is working on it as we speak."

"Let's order dinner," said Jason, "and while we're waiting, I'll tell you what my PI guy found out about the emails from Aaron to his father."

"I totally forgot about those," said Christie. "You were going to tell me something about them a few days ago but we got interrupted, I think."

"Well, they were pretty interesting. I don't have the details in front of me, but basically, Doyle had apparently told Aaron he was going to confront Michelle about something that had occurred long ago. Aaron was worried about how it would affect family relationships just before his cousin's wedding and begged him to hold off until after the wedding."

"Was there any hint of what this issue was all about?" asked Christie.

"Nothing specific. Neither Aaron nor Doyle ever stated what it was that had happened and it wasn't clear if Aaron even knew what it was, just that it was some big secret. He seemed to be appealing to his father not to say anything that would spoil Hailey's special day. His email to his father was the last of that series."

"But I want to know the rest of the story!" Christie wailed while the others laughed. "I feel like I'm in a never-ending saga with a white rabbit that keeps running in different directions. And I'm always too late."

"Hopefully, Conway will catch that bunny and put an end to this whole bit," said Jason.

"Speaking of Conway," said Christie, "he and Aaron were going to the hospital earlier today to look at the security tapes." She filled them in on the most recent failure to catch the bad guy. "He had suggested a few days ago that maybe Aaron and I had conspired to hurt Cameron, as if that were even possible. So I mentioned that Aaron, Doyle and Michelle were all in the same place, at the punch table, at the reception. Maybe they were doing some colluding."

"I don't know how he'd prove that. And colluding to do what?" Nathan gulped some of his drink and set the glass down with more force than necessary.

"Do you know for certain that Michelle told him to stay away?" Christie asked, recalling that she'd heard that comment from another source earlier.

"Maybe not in those exact words," said Nathan, "but Uncle Conan mentioned it to me at some point when I asked him about the wedding details. He was puzzled as to why the acrimony between them seemed to have worsened recently. Initially, it was caused by the high school dating drama that we all have heard about. He said they had a rough spot for a few months early in their marriage but attributed that to normal newlywed adjustment. They worked through that and resumed the status quo for the past twenty years until a month or two before the wedding. Michelle seemed to be getting more and more testy as the wedding day approached. He figured it was just the stress of the wedding itself because she wanted to impress the groom's family."

"But shouldn't the celebration have been all about Hailey and Ryan?" Christie asked.

"You don't know my Aunt Michelle well enough," said Nathan.

CHAPTER 41

*A*aron was sitting with his head in his hands, elbows on knees, on Christie's front doorstep when Jason and Christie drove up after dinner. They hurried up the sidewalk, concerned about his possible mental state.

Aaron's face was tear-stained when he looked up. "I think my dad is the one who tried to kill Cameron. I'm sure of it. I hate him."

Jason and Christie each took an arm and helped Aaron to his feet. He was wobbly and smelled of Scotch.

"Come inside, Aaron, and tell us what happened," said Christie, unlocking the door. Jason led Aaron to the armchair, where he sprawled out with arms hung over the sides. Stormy looked up from her bed next to the fireplace, stretched, and sauntered over to hop on Aaron's lap. It was as if she knew he needed some special attention. He managed a half-hearted smile and scratched her behind an ear.

"I'll brew some peppermint tea," said Christie. "It always works magic on frazzled nerves, according to my grandma Maude."

After a cup of hot tea and a couple of oatmeal raisin cookies,

Aaron seemed more revived. Christie and Jason sat on the sofa on the other side of the coffee table, waiting for him to talk about what had happened that evening.

"Okay, Aaron," said Christie. "Why do you think your dad was the one who tried to hurt Cameron?"

"You saw that photo with him and Michelle, didn't you?"

"Well, yes," Christie replied. "I'm guessing that Conway showed you the photo from the reception. Your dad appeared to be talking with her. Why do you think he was involved with harming Cameron?"

"Because he hates Cameron because he's gay. We're both gay. He has this fantasy that if Cameron is gone for good, I'll be his normal, heterosexual son. And he can go on his merry way and not have to admit that he's the father of a homosexual male. He's very angry about it. I've tried to explain that my being gay isn't a reflection of who or what *he* is, but he refuses to accept that view."

"That's not an uncommon situation for young men like you and Cameron," said Jason. "I see it frequently in my law office, especially when older parents are getting ready to write their wills."

"Yeah, well, I don't care about his money. I've got my own income. I hate him." Aaron's shoulders slumped even farther, if that were possible.

"He practically ignored me the whole time at the reception," Aaron went on. "Why did he bother to come? I've been trying to improve our relationship, and when I saw him at the wedding, I thought maybe it was a sign. And then…" He grabbed a wrinkled handkerchief from his back pocket and blew his nose.

"That hurts, pal," said Jason.

"I'm so sorry," said Christie. "But why do you think he tried to hurt Cameron? And how would he have done it?"

"He's prejudiced and narrow-minded is the 'why,' but I don't know the 'how.' That's what Conway is supposed to figure out."

Christie shrugged a shoulder. "What would he gain if he hurt your partner? You're already estranged, you've said."

"Yeah, but I've been emailing him and trying to get him to know Cameron a little better. He doesn't understand that being gay isn't caused by someone else. It's who I am. And he can't accept that." His eyes filled with tears, and he blew his nose again.

Jason nodded. "You'd think that in today's world, even someone like your father would know that people don't choose to be gay."

"And it's not like it's illegal or contagious," added Christie.

The three of them brooded in silence for a few moments. Christie poured more tea from the Delft blue and white teakettle she'd found in her grandma's kitchen. Aaron rubbed Stormy's belly. Jason tapped his fingers on the sofa.

"You're in a tough situation, obviously," said Christie. "At least you've got Cameron. Maybe your dad will come around sometime down the road, despite what he says now."

"Yeah. I'm most glad that Cameron's better. Dr. Pence says he can be discharged tomorrow, but he wants him to stay around here for a couple of days before we fly back to Goodyear, just in case."

"That sounds like a good idea," said Christie. "Would you like to bring him by the shop tomorrow on your way back to the hotel? I'd love to see him again before you leave town." She glanced at Jason. "Or join us out for dinner?"

Aaron brightened up. "I'm sure he'd like to do one or the other. I'll ask him tomorrow." He scooted Stormy from his lap, stood, and brushed black cat hair from his khakis. "I'm feeling a lot better. It's getting late, so I'll head back to the hotel."

"Are you okay to drive?" Jason, ever the attorney, asked as they walked together to the door.

Aaron chuckled. "Yeah, I'm good. Thanks for letting me get some stuff off my chest."

"We'll see you and Cameron tomorrow," said Christie. "Drive safely."

Christie and Jason watched from the front stoop as Aaron got into his car and drove down the street.

"It's awful to think that he believes his own father tried to hurt Cameron," said Christie once they were back inside, standing by the fireplace where Stormy had reclaimed her bed. "I wonder who the mystery woman is who visited him at the hospital. This is like trying to catch that elusive White Rabbit. Every clue ends up in a dead end."

Jason turned to face Christie, his arms around her shoulders. "Even in *Alice in Wonderland,* she eventually catches up to the White Rabbit." He kissed her on the forehead.

Christie giggled. "So you *do* believe in fairy tales, after all."

CHAPTER 42

The sun shone brightly Wednesday morning, causing the dew to sparkle on the flowers and shrubs in Christie's yard. She stood on the back porch admiring the view while holding Stormy in one arm and a mug of steaming coffee in the other hand. "Surely everything will be all right, won't it, Stormy? On a day like today, it's hard to believe there can be any malice in the world. Perhaps Conway will catch that White Rabbit, and I can stop worrying about my shop." She took a big breath of the fresh morning air, hugged her cat a little tighter, and went back inside.

Business was brisk that morning. Christie wondered if it was the weather itself that encouraged the flurry of customers who came in to buy cards, gift items, and the occasional pre-made bouquet from the display in the cooler. While Aunt Doris was busy creating floral arrangements to fulfill orders, including four more from fellow business owners, Christie focused on making bouquets to put in the cooler for walk-in customers. She made them in a variety of styles and colors with a range of prices, mostly on the lower side. This was her opportunity to experiment with ideas she'd found in magazines or online. And to play with her imagination to come up with something truly original.

She was busy at the register when Aaron and Cameron entered the shop just before noon. Cameron looked thinner than he had at the reception but was smiling broadly. Aaron had his arm around his partner's shoulder as they walked toward Christie. As they strolled through the retail part of the flower shop, Cameron's eyes moved from one display to another before finally landing on Christie herself.

"Everything in here is beautiful," he said, holding his hands to his chest. "I can see why Hailey asked you to do the flowers for her wedding."

"Why, thank you, Cameron," said Christie, choosing to keep the truth to herself.

"I'd love to know how you create such loveliness."

"Well, let's go into our workroom." Christie motioned to the back room. Cameron walked past her to the flower room in the back, where Doris was making a tabletop arrangement in a shallow container for someone's birthday. Her fingers flew as she snipped stems and inserted blooms and foliage into the green florist foam in the sage-green oval ceramic bowl.

"Do you think I could learn to do something like that?" Cameron directed his question to Doris.

She nodded and handed him a couple of stems of eucalyptus. "Of course. Let's see what you would do with these." She stepped aside and allowed him the freedom to place the silvery green foliage wherever he liked. She smiled and clapped her hands. "Very nice, young man. You seem to have an eye for beauty and balance."

Cameron beamed. "Thank you. I might look into taking some classes when we get back home." He peeked into the display case as he walked back toward Aaron and Christie. He pointed at an ikebana-style bouquet and said, "That looks very much like the flowers that the volunteer woman brought to me. Aaron, look at this and see if you agree."

Aaron and Christie crossed the room. "Yes, Cameron, it does." He turned to Christie. "Do you provide flowers for the hospital?"

"Not directly, but I know some of my bouquets get delivered to patients. I don't make anything for their gift shop, however. Do you happen to have a picture of the bouquet? If you do, I can tell whether or not it came from here."

"Even better," said Aaron. "It's in the car. It was still nice enough to enjoy one more day."

He returned a few minutes later carrying a somewhat worse-for-wear bouquet that was good for maybe another day or two, max.

Christie gasped. "That's definitely one of mine. I made it earlier this week." She called to her aunt. "Aunt Doris, do you remember who bought this one?"

Doris scurried from the workroom and squinted at the squat vase with the bedraggled flowers. She shook her head. "I didn't sell that one myself. Heather was helping at the time and rang it up. Maybe she'll remember."

Christie took a photo with her cell. "She's coming in after school today. I'll ask her then."

Doris reached out to take the vase from Aaron. "Let me fix that up for you."

Aaron asked, "Do you think this might have been the person who caused Cameron to have the relapse a couple of days ago?"

"Maybe. Can you describe her?" she asked Cameron, a surge of electricity running through her as she thought of white rabbits.

Cameron closed his eyes momentarily. "She was pretty, maybe the age of my mom, and had blond hair. At least, I think it was blond. Maybe it was light brown. Anyway, she was wearing a hat, too. It had a full brim, not like a baseball cap. It seems so unusual for ladies to wear actual hats nowadays, so it caught my attention." He shrugged. "That's all I can remember. I told the police chief the same thing."

"That's great, Cameron," said Christie. "I'll talk with the chief, too, to see if he has any leads."

Aaron put his hand on Cameron's shoulder. "Are you ready to go, Buddy? I don't want to wear you out on your first day out of the hospital."

Cameron reached out to shake Christie's hand; she leaned over and hugged him instead. "You take care. I hope you get all the way well so you can learn more about arranging flowers."

Doris rushed up with the newly improved flower bouquet. "Now you can enjoy them for a while longer," she said as she handed the flowers to Aaron.

Christie and Doris stood side by side, arms across each other's back, and watched the two young men leave the shop and get into Aaron's rental BMW.

"Who do you think that woman might have been?" Christie asked her aunt. "Do you know anyone who still wears a hat around here?"

Doris snorted. "I can't remember the last time I saw a woman with a hat on her head, except at last summer's rodeo. And those were all cowboy hats. None of the ladies wear a hat to church these days, not even at St. Thomas Catholic Church."

"I'm not optimistic that Heather will know who it was that purchased that bouquet, but I can hope," said Christie with a sigh. "And even then, I don't know what Conway can or will do about it because there's no way to prove she did anything more than purchase the flowers."

CHAPTER 43

"Heather, I'm so glad to see you," said Christie when the teenager popped into the shop at three thirty.

Heather, taken aback at the unusually peppy greeting, said, "Why? What's going on?"

Christie pulled out her phone and opened the photo of Cameron's bouquet. "Do you remember selling these flowers earlier this week?" She zoomed in for better detail.

Heather peered at the image and nodded. "Of course. I sold it to Mrs. Carnine."

"Are you sure of that name?"

"Well, yeah. Her son Luke is in a couple of my classes at school. Why?"

"Was she wearing a hat?"

"Yes, as a matter of fact, she was. I remember commenting on it because it looked old-fashioned, and she told me she'd just bought it at Sally's, the vintage store down the street." Heather looked at Christie with a frown. "Why? What's with the twenty questions?"

"Are you absolutely sure it was Mrs. Carnine? It's important."

"Yes, I'm sure. I remember being a little worried about the price because it was more expensive than the other bouquets, but Mrs. Carnine just smiled and paid cash for it. She didn't even use a card like most women do for something over twenty dollars." She put her hands on her hips and asked again, "Why? What's so important about those flowers?"

Christie hugged Heather and said, "I can't tell you yet for sure, but it might have something to do with Cameron Collins getting sick at the hospital. I'll explain later."

Heather shrugged and flounced to the workroom, where she donned a work apron.

Christie called Conway, who answered after a single ring. "What is it today, Christie?" He growled into her ear.

"I know who purchased the flowers that were delivered to Cameron at the hospital, but I can't prove that she delivered them herself."

"Who is it?"

Christie shared what Heather had told her.

"Do you have any contact information for her?"

"No, but she has at least one child attending White Castle High School. I'm sure you could get her phone number from the school." Christie glanced at the time. "There should be someone in the office until at least four o'clock if I remember correctly."

Conway exhaled loudly. "Tell you what. I'll contact her and see what she has to say. I hope it's not another goose chase, for your sake."

"Will you let me know what you find out?" Christie crossed her fingers.

"You know this is still part of a police investigation, so it depends on what she says."

"I understand," said Christie. "One more thing. Cameron and Aaron came by a few minutes ago. He said the lady who visited him was wearing a hat, just like the woman who bought the bouquet. I don't know if the lady in the video footage was wearing one, but if she was, it could be the same woman. Anyway, thank you for listening. And good luck."

Christie held the phone in her hand for a moment, sighed, and put it back in her pocket. Her aunt looked up from the workroom and, seeing the frown on her niece's face, said, "I suppose he said something less than what you hoped. Is that right?"

Christie nodded, a chagrinned smile on her face. "Sometimes I feel like Conway and I are friends. After all, I did help him solve that old murder last fall. And at other times, it seems more like we're sparring partners. And I'm usually the one who loses the match."

Doris clucked her tongue. "That's usually how it goes when there's an active investigation going on. Even though there's been no murder—thankfully—someone appears to have attempted to harm or kill that young man. I know you're still worried about your shop's reputation, as am I if the gossip mongers have their way."

"Business this week feels pretty normal, but that's partly because of the other small business owners supporting me with flower orders. But that can't go on forever." Stormy hopped down from her perch and rubbed her head against Christie's arm, purring loudly as she did so. At least her cat still liked her.

"Well, Honey, in small towns like White Castle, I think the local people are going to give you more support because they know who you are, as well as your parents and even your grandma Maude. And everybody knows that newspapers everywhere lean toward the sensational side to sell papers."

"I sure hope you're right, Auntie. My retirement account isn't looking very healthy yet."

The front door chimed the arrival of a customer, much to Christie's relief.

"Mrs. Fremmerlid!" Christie exclaimed at the sight of her

former high school English teacher. "I was thinking of you a few days ago when I talked to Missy."

"Missy? Missy Stewart? So you must have tracked her down after all."

Christie grinned. "Yes, I did. I'm sorry I didn't think to call you to tell you right away. It was right after you called to place that order for the flowers for the newspaper office. Anyway, thanks to you, I was able to connect her with her former beau, Brian Stone and their daughter, Lynette. You were correct in your guess that she was pregnant when she left town all those years ago."

"I didn't realize you had detective skills, young lady. Has she moved back here to town?"

"No, but she and Brian are getting married in White Castle in September, and she asked me to do the flowers for the wedding." Christie clasped her hands together, and then her face fell. "If I still have a business, that is."

Mrs. Fremmerlid moved closer to give her former student a hug. "Now, you don't go listening to that scuttlebutt out there. Most of the people who live here know you aren't responsible for people getting sick or dying just because of your flowers. They're just waiting for the police chief to get to the bottom of that young man being poisoned."

"*If* he ever gets to the bottom of it." Christie felt a prickle of fear despite the reassurances from both her former teacher and aunt. "And it's a small town, Mrs. Fremmerlid. What if my business can't survive the gossip? Or what if Chief Conway comes to the wrong conclusion because of pressure from people demanding that he close the case?"

"You just be patient, Christie. And carry on. Now, how about helping me pick out a pretty gift for my neighbor's birthday? Maddie Young turns eighty years young tomorrow, and the ladies in the condo are having a surprise party for her."

While Christie wrapped the boxed angel figurine in floral

paper, she asked Mrs. Fremmerlid how her book was coming along. The retired English teacher had told her the previous fall that she was writing a romance novel, of all things.

"How nice of you to ask, Christie," she exclaimed. "As a matter of fact, I decided to write a story about two young lovers who were tragically separated at a young age and then found each other later in life."

Christie grinned. "Just like Missy and Brian. How clever."

CHAPTER 44

ason called a few minutes after Christie arrived home. "Has Nathan called you yet?"

"No. Why would Nathan be calling me?"

"I thought he might tell you that he heard back from Sean about those cell phone calls that he had traced to Conan Starr's account."

"I wouldn't expect him to report back to me," said Christie, "but I hope he talked to Conway. I know they had a conversation about the Omega plant phone calls earlier. Did he give you any specifics?" She stooped to pick up Stormy, who was trying to get her attention about it being dinner time.

"Not really, because it's still an official government investigation, but he hinted that he'd all but verified who had access to the phone."

"Hm. I don't understand why he wouldn't just ask Conan about the phone if it's his account."

"He said he did and Conan didn't know anything about it. Someone else opened a second account with a different cell phone company without his knowledge or permission."

"Is that what Sean was able to determine with his telecommunications network?"

"Yes, and Nathan was planning to meet with Conway to share what he'd learned from Sean."

Christie glanced at the time. "It's probably too late for them to be meeting now, but maybe they already met earlier today. What time did Nathan tell you that news?"

"He called me about three this afternoon. He was going to call Conway right after we got off the phone."

"Even if Sean was able to identify who was using that phone account, it wouldn't tell him what the conversations were about, would it?"

"No, but it gives Conway a reason to talk to the account holder," said Jason. "Nathan had given him permission to follow up on the most recent calls to the nuclear plant, if you recall."

"But I don't see how that helps. Conan already passed the information about the call on his personal work phone to the police."

"It gives him leverage, Christie. It's illegal to make threats to a nuclear plant, however innocuous they may seem. Conway can use that angle to squeeze information out of the caller and hopefully find out who's behind the whole scheme."

"Oh. Now I get it. Nathan is hoping to identify the mastermind."

"Yes, Christie. Exactly."

"When I talked to Conway late this afternoon he didn't mention any of this. But of course, he wouldn't because it doesn't have anything to do with his other case."

"You mean the wedding reception case?"

"Yes," said Christie. "I found out today that Cameron's visitor bought the flowers from my shop, and Heather knew the lady's name. So I called Conway and asked if he would talk to the woman. He didn't sound hopeful about it helping much, but he indicated he'd do it."

"It sounds like he might be able to close two cases if Sean's information pans out in addition to finding out who the mystery woman is."

"That would be nice. Hey. I promised my mom I'd come over for dinner. I'm going to be late if I don't hustle, and I still need to feed Stormy."

"Okay. Call me later if you hear from Conway. I want to know what he found out from your mystery woman."

THE BLENDED AROMAS of warm bread and chicken marsala wafted from the kitchen when Christie arrived at her parents' home. After quick hellos and hugs, Thomas O'Mara poured glasses of a ruby-red Italian Barolo. He had become quite the aficionado of Italian wines recently and enjoyed finding something new to try. At the dinner table, Christie's mom, Maureen, who was Irish through and through, served a marsala as tasty as any Italian woman could. The chicken was tender, and the delicate marsala wine sauce was perfect. The crisp green salad and garlic French bread were the perfect accompaniments. And the Italian Barolo wine was excellent.

Christie enjoyed the banter at the dinner table with her mom and dad. After catching up on the latest family news, Christie asked if her mom had heard anything around the hospital recently about the poisoning case. Mrs. O'Mara volunteered at the local hospital and frequently heard stories about interesting patients, although names were never revealed in those tales.

"Are you asking me because you're still worried that it might affect your business?"

"Basically, yes," Christie admitted. "It doesn't take much these days for bad news, whether or not it's true, to hurt a reputation. What are you hearing from the other volunteers?"

"Well, honey, everyone agrees that the man who got sick

must have eaten something. We all agree that the flowers were innocent bystanders. I mean, how can you get sick from a bouquet of pretty blossoms?" Maureen smiled and raised her shoulders while Christie listened. Her mother's comment about the food triggered a reminder to ask Conway if the food at the reception had ever been tested. Or had he focused entirely on her flowers because of the initial report of belladonna-like symptoms?

"That's good to hear," said Christie. "The problem is that food poisoning causes diarrhea more often than it would trigger the symptoms suffered by the victim in question, but I'm glad to know that at least some people think the flowers are innocent. I'd rather blame the food, myself."

Thomas raised his glass. "I'll drink to that." They all laughed, the somber tone having been lifted by the simple toast.

In the kitchen, where Christie was helping her mom with the dishes and clean-up, Maureen asked, "When are we going to see your friend Jason again? He's a nice young man."

When Christie didn't immediately answer, Maureen added, "You could bring him over here for Sunday dinner sometime."

"Thanks, Mom. I'll check with him and see if he has any free weekends coming up."

"No pressure, Christie. It's just an idea." Maureen dished up a leftover dinner for her daughter and put a few kitty treats in a plastic sandwich bag for Stormy.

"I know," said Christie as she collected her jacket. "I appreciate the thought, but I don't want Jason to think we're ganging up on him."

"He's a very nice young man, and he seems to like you." She winked.

Christie hugged her mom and kissed her on the cheek, her own cheeks reddening. "Thanks for the dinner and Stormy's treats."

. . .

BACK HOME IN her own cozy living room, Christie sipped on a glass of wine and listened to a recording of Chopin preludes on her Bose CD player. "I should start taking piano lessons," she told her kitty. "Mom tried to tell me when I was a kid that I'd be sorry I didn't continue them when I quit lessons in fifth grade. I guess she was right."

Stormy lay curled in her lap and purred her agreement.

As the music played in the background, Christie's mind wandered back to the mystery of Cameron and his illness. She picked up a notebook lying on the coffee table in front of her and started listing the facts and assumptions, beginning with the wedding reception itself. The fact that Cameron collapsed at the reception was followed by a multitude of guesses, some of which had been proven wrong and others correct. There didn't seem to be any way to verify what actually happened at the punch table or what was in the package that Aaron picked up the day of the wedding.

As Christie listed more unknowns, she puzzled again over Aaron's strange reaction to Conway's telling him that the jacket had been found. At the time, she thought he might have had an emotional attachment to the missing jacket, perhaps because Cameron had worn it, but was it possible he already knew that traces of belladonna would be found? If so, maybe he made such a big fuss over needing to find the jacket so he could destroy the evidence himself. When the forensics lab found evidence of the belladonna, he had to cover his tracks. And…he would need to find a way to blame someone else.

She quickly reached for her phone to place a call to Conway, getting a disgruntled eye from Stormy as the movement temporarily repositioned her. But Christie didn't apologize to the kitty—she had an idea.

CHAPTER 45

I wish it were a Friday, Christie thought to herself as she entered her shop Thursday morning and greeted her aunt. She lifted Stormy to her observation post and grabbed a work apron from one of the pegs in the workroom. Doris was already working on an order for two dozen fresh flower bouquets for a big fundraising event that evening. Thankfully, the warehouse order had been delivered the previous afternoon. which allowed Christie and Doris to work on them first thing in the morning. Heather was on tap to deliver them after school, which gave them about six hours to complete the task.

"Who did you say ordered these flowers?" Doris asked while snipping stems to the correct length for the squatty bowls. The vases were to be in the centers of round tables with a maximum height of twelve inches so they wouldn't interfere with conversation across the tables. "There aren't many calls for this quantity of tabletop decorations around here. Although it's the second order this week if you count the PTA shindig."

"The local Red Hat Society is hosting a regional convention at the largest hotel in Ionia," said Christie. "One of the women on the decorating committee is a good friend of my mom and she talked to the other members about offering me the contract for the job. After some discussion, they decided to support my business instead of trying to do it on their own. They figured that by the time they bought the materials at retail prices, it would be more cost-effective to hire it out, especially when they would have to decorate that number of tables."

"Good decision," said Aunt Doris. "I'm glad there are only twenty-four tables, myself." She dried her hands and wiped her forehead with the towel.

The women worked side by side, snipping stems and foliage to the correct length and inserting the blooms and greenery into the bowls.

Christie held one in her hands. "This one is done. What do you think, Auntie?"

Doris nodded and placed the completed arrangement in a shallow cardboard box for transporting in the van, then into the cooler, where it would stay until it was time for delivery.

"What's the latest on Conway?" her aunt asked. "You haven't mentioned him yet today."

"I talked to him yesterday about the lady with the hat, as you know, but nothing since. He kinda blew me off."

"Oh, Christie. I'm sure he knows you're only trying to help."

"That's sure not how it feels." Christie looked up briefly to see who was entering the shop when the chime tinkled its happy sound. "There he is now. He almost looks like he's smiling. Do you think that's a smile, Auntie?"

Doris glanced at the police chief as he strolled through the front of the shop toward the two women. "I do believe he looks happier than usual."

Christie wiped her hands on a towel and whipped off her apron, tossing it on the end of the worktable.

"Hey, Conway." Christie offered a dry hand. "You're smiling. Did you catch the White Rabbit?" She stood at one end of the counter, leaning on one elbow. Conway stood at the other end. Stormy jumped down from her shelf to get a couple of ear scratches from the chief.

Conway cleared his throat. He shook his head and gave Christie a funny look. "Rabbit? No, it's not hunting season. I just came from the station where I met with Cameron and Aaron. Cameron was able to identify Pamela Carnine as the lady who delivered the flowers, but as far as I can tell, she's only guilty of the delivery itself."

"I don't understand what you mean by that."

"She told me she was doing a favor for a friend who had given her the muffin and orange juice in a small gift bag and asked her to buy a nice bouquet as well to deliver to the hospital."

Christie furrowed her brow. "Did her friend tell her to come *here* for the flowers?"

"I don't think so, but who else in town sells nice bouquets?" he said with a sly wink. "Anyway, she wasn't lying about being a volunteer at the hospital, although she wasn't working her shift when she visited Cameron."

"So, did she tell you who the favor was for?"

"As a matter of fact, she did. You realize, of course, that she didn't know anything about why Cameron was in the hospital or that he later had a bad reaction. She was in and out of the room in a matter of a few minutes."

"Understood. But who was the favor for? Or can you tell me?"

"I know who it was, but I can't tell you just yet. I haven't talked with the woman, but I've asked her to meet me at the station a little later this morning. She wanted to bring her husband with her and needed to give him time to get back in town."

"Will you tell me if I guess correctly?"

"No, Christie. Don't even try. You'll have to trust me for a bit longer while I follow up on some related business. I just wanted to thank you for the information on who bought that bouquet. ” Conway pushed himself away from the counter and put his hat back on his head.

He looked over Christie's shoulder where Doris was still working—all ears, of course. "Hey Aunt Doris. That's a lot of flowers. Are there any of those belladonna lilies?"

She waved a damp towel at him and snorted.

After Conway left, Christie could hardly settle down to help her aunt finish the remaining arrangements. "Do you want to guess who the woman was, Aunt Doris?"

"I really don't know Pamela Carnine at all. I'm not sure I've ever seen her in here and she doesn't go to my church. So I haven't any idea who she runs with. Is her address on the order slip for the bouquet?"

With a little searching, Christie dug up the receipt for the order and determined Pamela lived in one of those newer gated developments out on the river.

Doris nodded. "If I had to guess, I'd say she might belong to the country club crowd out that way, but that's just a stab in the dark. Now, let's finish getting these orders done. It might get busy later today."

A steady stream of women purchased cards and gift items through the early afternoon. Nicer weather definitely drew customers to downtown Main Street, where they browsed from store to store. A couple of men stopped by late in the day and purchased ready-made floral gifts. *Probably for anniversaries,* Christie thought to herself as she helped each of them select flowers from the cooler. The "Happy Anniversary" cards selected by each of the men confirmed her suspicion.

She leaned on the counter and watched the second man as he exited the shop. She found herself wondering if she would ever be married and if her husband would race to a flower shop to buy a last-minute gift before taking her out for a nice dinner. She was still lost in thought when Heather came in through the back door, ready to load her van with the flowers for delivery.

"Hi, Christie. Hi Aunt Doris," Heather said cheerfully. She walked into the workroom and peeked into the cooler. "Looks like you've been busy. Those are really pretty. Where are they going?"

"Up the highway to Ionia, to the new Highwayman Hotel. The Red Hat women are having a convention in the hotel's new conference center."

"Ah. That explains why they're all red and pink and purple."

"Don't forget the white baby's breath," added Aunt Doris with a chuckle.

"Before you start loading them up, I have a question for you," said Christie. "Do you happen to know who Luke Carnine's parents are friends with?"

"Not really," she replied, "but he's best friends with Isaac Palmer, and I know their dads play golf together at the country club. Why?"

"Just curious," said Christie.

Heather looked at her boss with narrowed eyes. "Does this have anything to do with the flowers I rang up for her earlier this week?"

"Maybe," said Christie. She wanted to blurt out the rest of the story but bit her tongue instead and said, "I'll help you load the van while Aunt Doris keeps an eye on the store."

CHAPTER 46

Christie and Jason met Anita and Nathan at the Silver Spoon Saloon for dinner. The four had become fast friends during the time that Anita and Nathan had been dating.

"How long will you be in White Castle, Nathan?" Christie asked while waiting for their wine to be served. "It feels like you fit right into our little community."

Nathan pursed his lips and glanced at Anita. "I'm afraid I'll be heading back to the office in Arlington, Texas, next week."

Christie noticed a wince of discomfort cross Anita's face.

"I told Anita on our way over here that the mini-crisis at Omega is over, and my boss has recalled me for my real job." He reached over and squeezed Anita's hand.

"That's good news, ending the crisis, that is," said Christie. "What did you discover? Can you tell us?"

"I can tell you some of it, but you'll have to wait for official channels to release the names that fill in the blanks." He paused while the waitress set the bottle of Chianti and four glasses on the table.

"I'll come back for your order in a few moments," the waitress said after filling the stemless wine glasses.

"Let's toast to solving the Omega mystery," said Jason, raising his glass. "Although it's not the end of all mysteries," he added with a chuckle.

The others groaned and joined in with, "Here, here."

Nathan took a couple of swallows of the dry, ruby-red wine. "Sean, the future son-in-law of your friend Missy, produced evidence that proved the calls to my uncle Conan's office phone were made by someone known to him. I had to call the federal police in because of the nature of the calls that were made to a governmental agency."

"Has this person been arrested, then?" Christie asked, dying to know who it was.

"Yes. And, no, I won't tell you anymore. You'll know soon enough. I promise."

"It can't be soon enough for me," said Christie. "It seems like my life has been on hold these past two weeks between the nuclear plant and the Starr family wedding and Cameron's poisoning at the reception. My sixth sense tells me it's all connected, and now you tell me I have to wait some more." She made a face and took a couple of big swallows of her wine.

Christie's phone buzzed on the table. Conway's name lit up the screen. "And now it's Conway again. He's the one holding up the other half of my life." She pressed the green icon. "Christie here. Do you have good news, Chief?" She furrowed her brow. "Sure. I'm at the Silver Spoon Saloon with some friends. See you in a few."

"He's coming here?" Jason asked. "He must have something pretty big to track you down in the evening."

"I hope he leaves his wrist cuffs in his cruiser," Christie said drolly. "I'd hate to be arrested in public. Even if it's just a bar."

The waitress returned to take dinner orders. Jason ordered a second bottle of wine to go with the burgers, fries and onion rings.

A few minutes passed. Christie tapped her foot nervously

under the table. Jason told a lawyer joke. Then Nathan spotted Conway in the doorway and stepped on Christie's tapping foot under the table with his size-eleven shoe.

"Hello, Chief," said Nathan as Conway approached. "Do you need to speak to Christie privately? The rest of us can disappear for a while."

Conway grabbed a chair from a neighboring table and straddled it, facing the foursome. He placed his eve-present hat on the table in front of him. "Nope. It'll all be in the news on the radio in the morning anyway."

Conway continued, saying, "I'll start with the calls to the nuclear plant, seeing as Nathan is here, too. Once we identified the cell phone that had made the calls to Conan Starr's private office phone, it was easy to have Detective McAvoy make a call and see who answered."

"How long ago did you do that?" asked Christie, recalling that Nathan had known the call had been made from a cell phone at least the week before.

"Well, we didn't have the actual phone number until a couple of days ago when Sean, your communications expert friend, was able to share it with the feds, who gave us permission to follow up." He looked directly at Christie. "It was your friend Doyle Starr, Aaron's father."

Christie scoffed. "Doyle? I wouldn't exactly call him my friend, and why would he be calling the nuclear plant anonymously in the first place?"

"It turns out that Doyle picked up a burner phone that he used to place the calls to Conan and registered it under Conan's name. One of his motives for the phone was to make the threats to Conan. Doyle saw his brother's success, his family, and jealousy drove him to threaten Conan's base—his plant—so he made those calls. He thought if he could create enough noise, the investigators would actually find something they could pin on his brother. Or at least put his position at the plant at risk. He also made a couple of calls using the same phone to Michelle, trying to blackmail her."

"Blackmail her for what?" asked Jason. "What did she have to hide?"

"Nathan may already know this, but for the rest of you, Michelle had dated Doyle when they were in high school. Somewhere along the way, she fell in love with his older brother Conan and eventually married him."

Nathan waved off the waitress who was approaching the table.

"Apparently, and Michelle told me this," Conway went on, "she had a brief fling with Doyle while she and Conan were engaged—he was out of town for several weeks—and had immediate remorse. She never told Conan and has been the good wife ever since, she says. Anyway, Doyle got the idea somehow that Hailey, Michelle and Conan's oldest child, was born of that fling and was threatening to tell Conan about it. Michelle said the dates weren't even remotely possible, but Doyle wouldn't let it go."

"Something like that could ruin your day," said Jason.

"In that case, I can understand why Michelle told Doyle to stay away from the wedding, but what does that have to do with Aaron and Cameron?" asked Christie. "What was that all about?"

"I believe you've already heard that Doyle had a problem with his son Aaron being gay. And didn't approve of his relationship with Cameron. So when Cameron collapsed, it looked like it was all about the gay thing."

"But it wasn't?" asked Christie.

"No. It was about Nathan."

"Me?" Nathan's mouth fell open.

Conway nodded. "Yeah. Shocking, isn't it? I spent an hour with Aaron and Cameron just before I came over here, and I think I have the story straight. Anyway, although Doyle's not thrilled with his son being gay, more than that, he hates Arthur, Nathan's father, who *is* a homophobe. Aaron had heard all his life that Uncle Arthur was corrupt and untrustworthy. Plus, Arthur himself made it clear he was a gay-hater. Aaron got it in his head that Nathan was just like him—corrupt and untrustworthy and a homophobe. Another factor—Aaron and Cameron are members of an activist group that targets nuclear facilities, as Jason's PI had discovered. For the most part, Aaron was the main instigator behind the complaints about Omega just because of his anti-nuclear philosophy. Cameron was in on it only because of Aaron's strong interest. Anyway, Aaron was trying to move up to a higher position in the group. When he heard that the cousin he considered corrupt anyway was about to investigate a nuclear facility run by their mutual uncle, he figured corruption was in full swing. I mean, it looked like an obvious conflict of interest to him. He believed that Nathan was in his uncle Conan's pocket, so to speak, and decided to discredit both of them, which would make him look good in the eyes of the other activists."

"But killing me seems extreme," said Nathan, "especially if it meant Aaron were to end up in jail."

Conway continued. "He wasn't trying to kill you, actually. What he'd used would normally just make someone ill for some time. It would require interactions with other substances to make it lethal. He just wanted to make you sick enough to get you out of the way of the investigation and end the perceived nepotism. He thought the NRC might even think Conan poisoned his own nephew to prevent the discovery of the so-called inconsistencies that had been reported by Aaron in the first place. That would maybe force the NRC to bring in the big guns to do a more thorough investigation and would at least halt production at the nuclear plant for the short term."

"That seems shortsighted to me," said Jason.

"But how did Cameron end up being poisoned if Nathan was the target?" asked Christie.

Conway nodded grimly. "Cameron explained to me that he was distraught when Aaron told him he was going to invite Nathan over to make peace over a cocktail. He knew Aaron disliked Nathan, and he expected another scene. Michelle had given Aaron a tray with three glasses of punch. Two were spiked —the glasses with the berries at the bottom—and one was not. While Aaron went over to invite Nathan to join them, his own glass in hand, Cameron quickly drank the other glass of the spiked punch—the one intended for Nathan—and poured the non-alcoholic punch into the now-empty glass with the berries. Even though he typically didn't drink much, he knew from experience that he could have one drink without triggering a drug reaction. He said he just really wanted a bit of a bracer before more potential drama. What he didn't know was that Aaron had poured a vial of belladonna liquid—that's what was in the UPS package—into the other glass, the one he was going to offer to Nathan."

"Is that what Aaron was doing in the photo that we saw?" asked Christie.

"Very likely," replied Conway. "Then he slipped the empty vial into Cameron's jacket pocket—which is why the lab found the trace of belladonna—when he came back to the table. He adjusted Cameron's boutonniere to cover his action. And thought he'd gotten away with destroying the evidence. That's why he panicked when I told him we'd found the missing jacket or what was left of it. Christie called me last night and I agreed with her about the jacket being crucial to the evidence after all. When I talked with him just a bit earlier, he finally fessed up."

"Oh! How tragic," said Christie. "And Aaron didn't know, of course, that Cameron had switched the glasses."

"Correct," said Conway. "You may recall that Aaron said he went to get his car to leave right away. That was because he was expecting Nathan to collapse from the tainted drink, and he planned to be out of the building when that happened. When

Cameron wasn't waiting to be picked up at the door, he came back in and discovered Cameron on the floor and Nathan still standing. That's when he realized what might have happened."

"What about the empty vial? Why wasn't it in the jacket pocket?" asked Christie.

Conway said, "Our best guess is that it fell out somewhere along the way--maybe in the emergency room when they removed his clothing. And might not have even been noticed."

"I suppose that makes sense." said Christie, nodding. "Or it could have fallen out when he collapsed at the country club."

"That's another good idea," said Conway.

"So, are you thinking he was blaming anybody and everybody, including Christie and me, to deflect blame from himself?" asked Nathan.

"Yes, Nathan. Obviously, he was upset that he had accidentally poisoned his own partner. But you also had opportunity, though I was scratching my head for a motive." Conway stood to leave. "One more thing I want to say to Christie."

"Does it have to do with minding my own business?" Christie asked warily.

"Not at all, Christie," Conway replied. "You kept me on my toes with your questions. Without your persistence I might not have known about Mrs. Carnine or the package that contained the belladonna liquid that Aaron ordered."

Christie's face reddened. "I was only worried about how my business might be affected, and I knew Cameron's illness didn't really have anything to do with my flowers."

Conway put his hat back on his head and stood. "I need to take care of a few loose ends, but I wanted to let you know that I'm considering this case to be solved. Now, I hope you all have a good evening."

"Before you leave, I have to ask," said Jason, "being the attorney and all, if Doyle is in jail yet."

"He's awaiting transfer to a federal facility because of the threats to the nuclear plant, but he's in the county jail for the moment. Aaron is also facing charges, though we haven't sorted that out just yet. This isn't official, but I wouldn't be surprised to hear that he'll turn over information about the activist group and be given some leniency. After all, he is Cameron's primary care-giver, and his partner will need time to recover. I think that would trump his need to stay in the activist group."

"Do you have any other surprises to tell us?" asked Christie.

Conway shook his head, a half smile on his face. "Read tomorrow's paper."

CHAPTER 47

The sun seemed to shine more brightly than usual, the birds chirped their merriest, and even the grass looked greener in the lawns that Christie passed by on her way to her shop.

Aunt Doris noticed the bounce in Christie's step and the cheerfulness in her voice right away. "You're Miss Sweetness and Light today. What's happened?"

Christie lifted Stormy to her perch and smiled. "Conway finally solved his case yesterday. Which means I'm going to be in business in September for Missy's wedding and Leanne's, too."

Doris smiled. "I always knew it would turn out okay." She tossed the Friday morning issue of the *White Castle Gazette* on the counter in front of Christie.

Christie's Flowers Found Innocent read the headline above the fold on the front page. Christie quickly read the article, grinning as she did so. The reporter didn't report as much information as Conway had shared the previous evening, but she made it clear that the public was safe from murderous flowers.

Christie shared the additional details that she'd learned the previous evening. "I feel terrible for Aaron, although he may well deserve whatever's coming to him. I mean, he did try to poison his cousin, even if it was not meant to be lethal. Conway also said he thought Cameron was going to be okay after all."

"What about that relapse? Did his doctor ever figure that out?"

"Funny thing, kind of," said Christie. "Cameron's doctor had restarted that medicine for his condition, the one with all the food interactions and all. His chart hadn't been flagged in dietary yet so he accidentally was served pepperoni pizza for lunch that day. Cameron's memory hadn't cleared up entirely, so he didn't remember he was supposed to avoid eating pepperoni. According to Wikipedia, both the pepperoni and the cheese on his pizza were potential triggers for a reaction if he ate enough of them. Fortunately, it was a relatively minor reaction, and it got caught right away."

"I think I'd want to take a different medicine if it were me," said her aunt.

"I'm with you there." Christie picked up an order from the top of the small stack on the worktable and selected a mauve vase and a handful of stems for a cheerful birthday bouquet. "I still wonder who sent Pamela Carnine to deliver the items to Cameron in the hospital."

"Oh, I know that answer!" Doris looked at her, a smile on her face. "I called Pamela earlier on the pretense to be sure the flowers were satisfactory, and she explained she was just the middleman. I pressed her about it, and she said it was Michelle Starr who had her pick them up. Michelle told Pam she felt so bad about what happened to Cameron but didn't want to cause more drama by going herself, and, knowing Pam was a volunteer, asked her to take some treats and flowers to cheer him up."

Christie said, "I guess Michelle, even if she wasn't happy at the start about Aaron and Cameron attending, certainly tried to make things right. She offered an excuse for Aaron being late for the pictures, innocently suggested to Aaron that the three young men should make amends with the drinks, and then sent anonymous gifts to the stricken Cameron. All of that puts Michelle in a better light to me."

"So," said Aunt Doris, "that sounds like a happy ending for everyone—except Doyle and Aaron, of course. Although it looks like you won't be filling any more bouquet orders from the women's group for the newspaper."

"Oh, I'm just so grateful they did that. I can't help but think the editor will be a bit more careful in the future," said Christie.

While inserting several more stems and some greenery into the vase, Christie said, "Oh, there's one more thing. Michelle only considered a divorce to save face for Conan. She assumed that if Doyle's assertion came out about Hailey being Doyle's daughter, her husband might want a divorce. She finally told Conan the truth when he asked why she would even consider it. Turns out Doyle had bragged to him about it a long time ago, so he knew anyway, although he wasn't sure it was the truth. He'd given her the benefit of the doubt all these years. And had no desire for a divorce."

"He sounds like a good man," said Aunt Doris.

"I agree. Well, I'm glad it's all over. It's been a very long two weeks." Christie stepped back to admire her work. "Anita may be the only one who's not happy."

"Why would that be?" Aunt Doris asked as she stepped back to scrutinize a floral arrangement.

"You've heard me talk about her friend Nathan. They've been seeing each other while he's been in town the past six weeks doing the investigative work at the Omega plant. Now that his job is done here, he'll be heading back to Arlington, Texas. That's where his agency's regional headquarters office is."

"Texas is a long way away," acknowledged Aunt Doris. "But they can stay in touch with cell phones and texting, I suppose."

"True, but long-distance romances are hard to maintain, I've heard."

"Never tried one, honey, so I wouldn't know," Aunt Doris said soberly.

Christie finished the bouquet and placed it in the cooler for pick-up later that morning. When the shop phone rang, she said, "I'll get it. I already have dry hands.

"Christie's Flower Shoppe. How can I help you?" she answered cheerfully. "That sounds wonderful...I'd love to do that...Starting Monday?...Of course...Thank you so much. Have a wonderful weekend."

Christie replaced the handset and danced a little jig. "That was Deb at the bookstore. She decided to continue featuring one book every week that involves flowers and wants to have us provide a bouquet of flowers with a message every Monday."

"Explain, please," replied her aunt. "What kind of message?"

"You know, a message that the flowers imply that goes along with the title, and she'll tell us the book title in advance so we can order the right flowers."

"Did she tell you what book she's featuring next week?"

"Yes. *The Secret Garden* by Frances Hodgson Burnett. Do you think we can come up with something, Auntie?"

"I'll do a little research and make a list of the flowers we'll need. This will be fun."

The front door chimed, and Christie looked up to see Leanne and her mother enter the shop. She walked up to meet them and said, "I was just telling Aunt Doris that I need to start working on the details for your wedding in September. Shall we begin?"

THE END

ACKNOWLEDGMENTS

Books don't happen without a lot of help. Many thanks go to Sandra Herner, development editor extraordinaire, whom I "met" through Reedsy.com. She always makes my stories make more sense. Thank you!

Cover design credit goes to Damonza.com. They do amazing covers and are easy to work with. Even when I want just one more tiny change!

I was good in English when I was in school, but Kathleen Costello is even better. Her red pencil is found at kcostello@grammartogo.com.

My number one beta reader, Angela Thompson, brainstorms with me when I'm playing with plot elements or just need a shoulder when I'm stuck, stuck, stuck. She has read more pages than me, probably, when all is said and done.

And thank you to my husband, Steve Jones, for allowing me the time and space to write. And for carrying my business cards wherever we go. He's a gem!

ABOUT THE AUTHOR

PJ Peterson is the author of mysteries in two different series.

Killer Wedding is the second story in her Christie's Flower Shoppe Cozy Mystery series. You can be sure that another episode will follow Christie O'Mara and her shop cat, Stormy.

She also writes the Julia Fairchild Mystery series, featuring an amateur sleuth who happens to be a young internist as the protagonist. She says that her character is a younger, smarter version of herself. Dr. Fairchild debuted in *Blind Fish Don't Talk.*

PJ knew she wanted to be a doctor at the age of seven so she could "help people." Now a retired physician, she writes books to keep her brain busy. She hopes her stories help people now by keeping them entertained.

She welcomes reviews and visits to her webpage at http://www.pjpetersonauthor.com